JULES VERNE'S

20,000 LEAGUES UNDER THE SEA

A GRAPHIC NOVEL

BY CARL BOWEN &
JOSÉ ALFONSO OCAMPO RUIZ

D0972444

STONE ARCH BOOKS
A CAPSTONE IMPRINT

Graphic Revolve is published by Stone Arch Books
A Capstone Imprint
1710 Roe Crest Drive, North Mankato, Minnesota 56003
www.capstonepub.com

Cataloging-in-Publication Data is available at the Library
of Congress website.
Hardcover ISBN: 978-1-4965-0001-4
Paperback ISBN: 978-1-4965-0002-1

Summary: Scientist Pierre Aronnax and his trusty servant
set sail to hunt a sea monster. With help from Ned Land,
the world's greatest harpooner, the men soon discover
that the creature is really a high-tech submarine. To
keep this secret from being revealed, the sub's leader,
Captain Nemo, takes the men hostage. Now, each man
must decide whether to trust Nemo or try to escape this
underwater world.

Common Core back matter written by Dr. Katie Monnin.

Color by Benny Fuentes and Protobunker Studio

Designer: Bob Lentz
Assistant Designer: Peggie Carley
Editor: Donald Lemke
Assistant Editor: Sean Tulien
Creative Director: Heather Kindseth
Editorial Director: Michael Dahl
Publisher: Ashley C. Andersen Zantop

Printed in the United States of America in
Stevens Point, Wisconsin.
009859R

TABLE OF CONTENTS

ABOUT SUBMARINES

Many people believe Alexander the Great was the first person to journey underwater in a contained vessel. Legend says the Greek leader explored the Aegean Sea inside a glass barrel around 333 BC, more than 2,000 years ago.

Artist Leonardo Da Vinci, who painted the famous *Mona Lisa*, also worked on plans to build an underwater ship during the 1500s. However, Da Vinci kept his plans a secret because he feared the invention would eventually be used for war.

Less than 300 years later, Da Vinci's prediction came true. David Bushnell built the first submarine used for battle. The *Turtle*, as it was called, was made of wood, held one person, and could stay under the water for a half hour. On September 6, 1776, the American army used the *Turtle* against a British warship. The attack was unsuccessful.

During the Civil War, the United States Navy tested their first submarine. The *Alligator* measured 47 feet long and could hold more than 14 crew members. While being towed into battle in 1863, a storm sunk the sub off the coast of North Carolina. It has never been found.

Early subs were often powered by oars or hand-cranked propellers. The United States Navy launched the first nuclear-powered submarine in 1954. It was named the *Nautilus*, the same as Captain Nemo's underwater vessel. In 1958, the *Nautilus* became the first sub to cross beneath the North Pole.

Nuclear energy has since powered some of the fastest subs ever built, including Russia's Alfa class submarines. These subs could travel nearly 300 miles per hour!

On January 23, 1960, the *Trieste* became the deepest-diving underwater vessel ever built. The *Trieste* dove nearly 38,000 feet before reaching the floor of the Pacific Ocean.

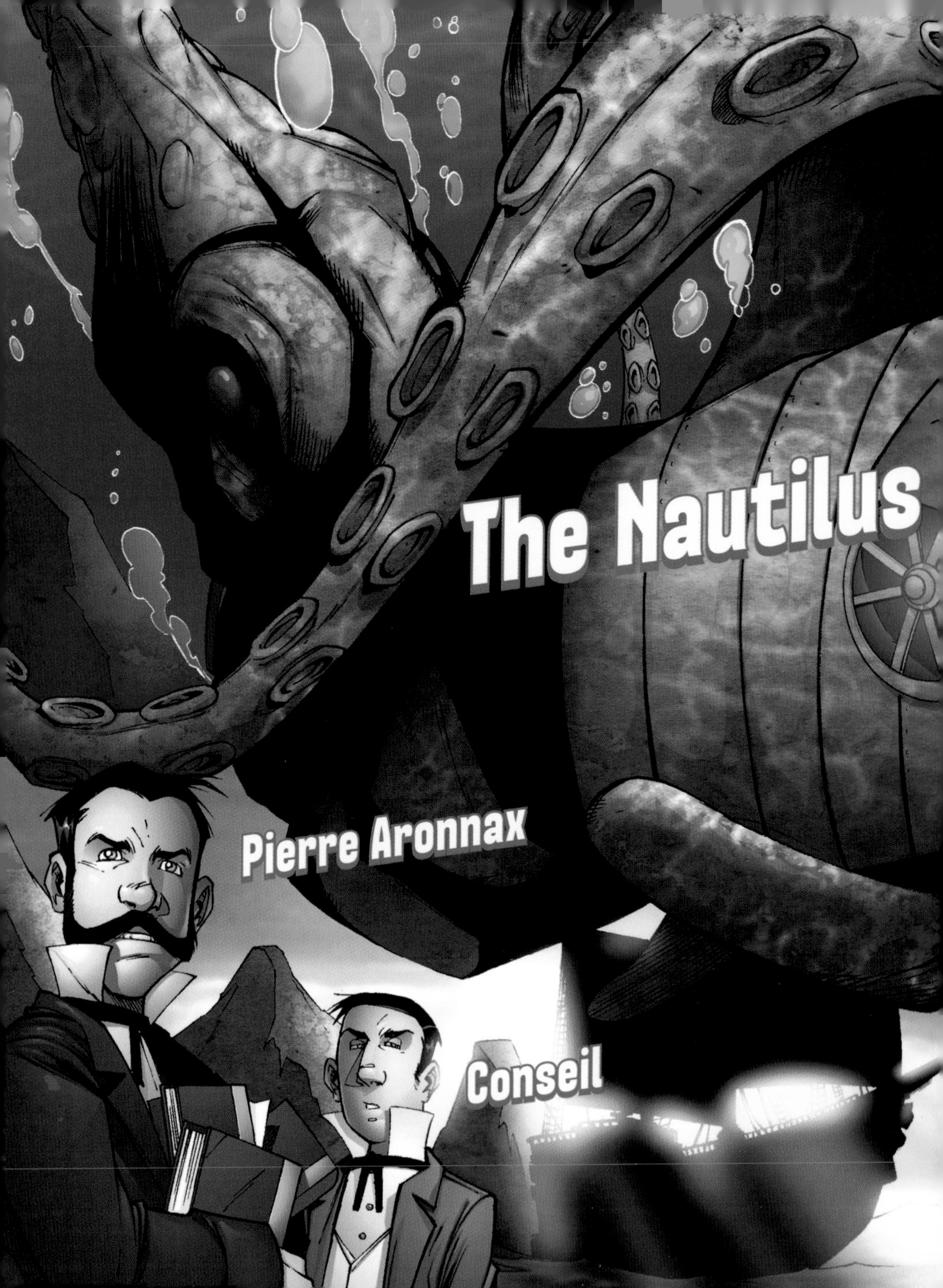

The Nautilus
Pierre Aronnax
Conseil

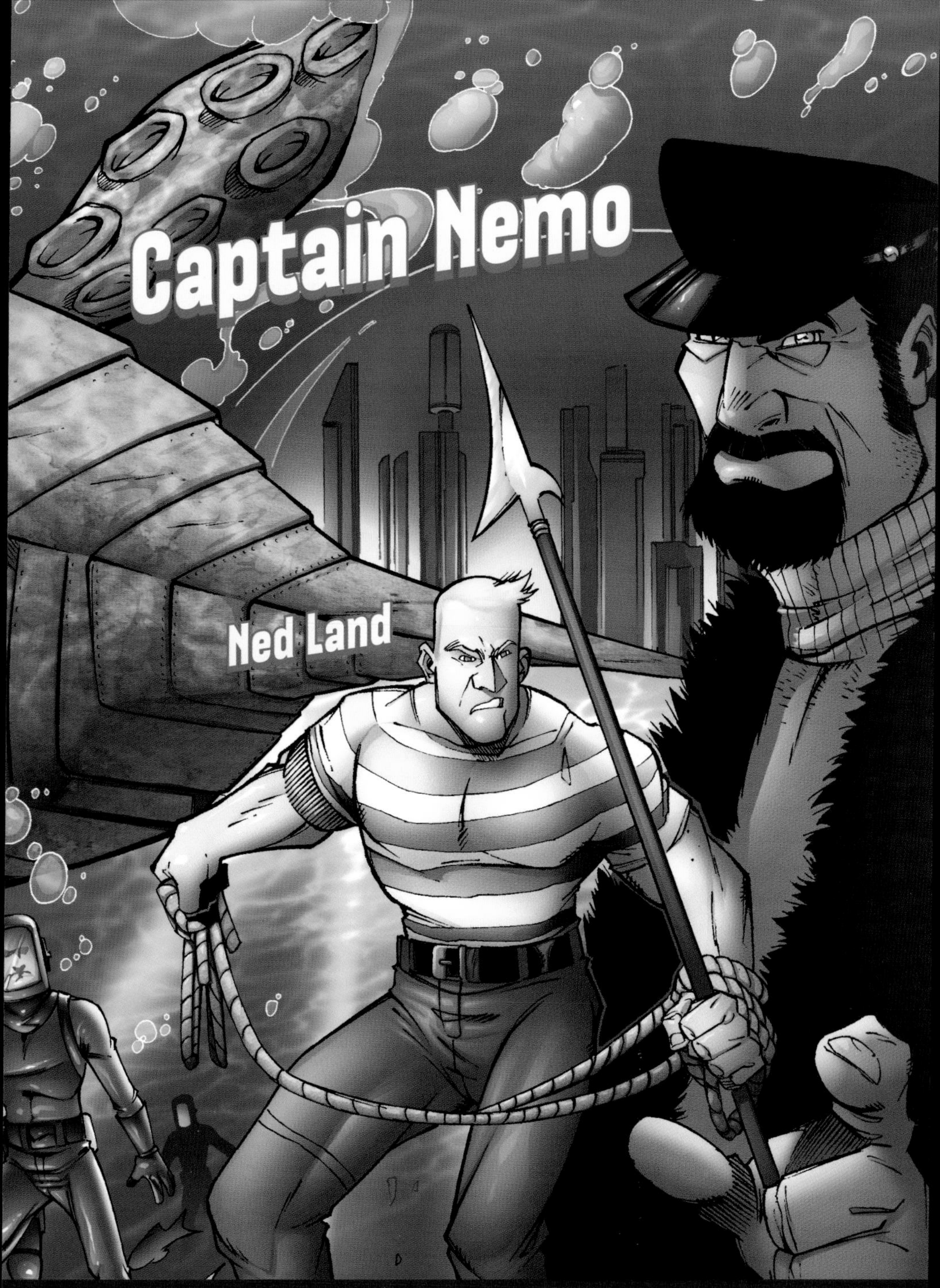
Captain Nemo
Ned Land

In 1866, sailors began to notice something strange in the seas.

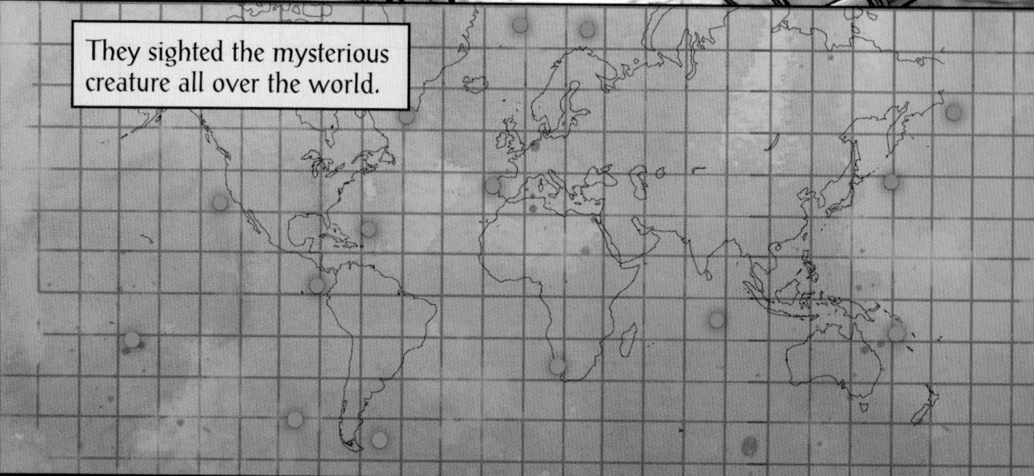

They sighted the mysterious creature all over the world.

At first, the strange mystery was exciting. But in 1867, the creature began to attack ships.

MONS[
SIGHTED AT

TERROR ON T[
HIGH SEAS !!

According to eastern the last week

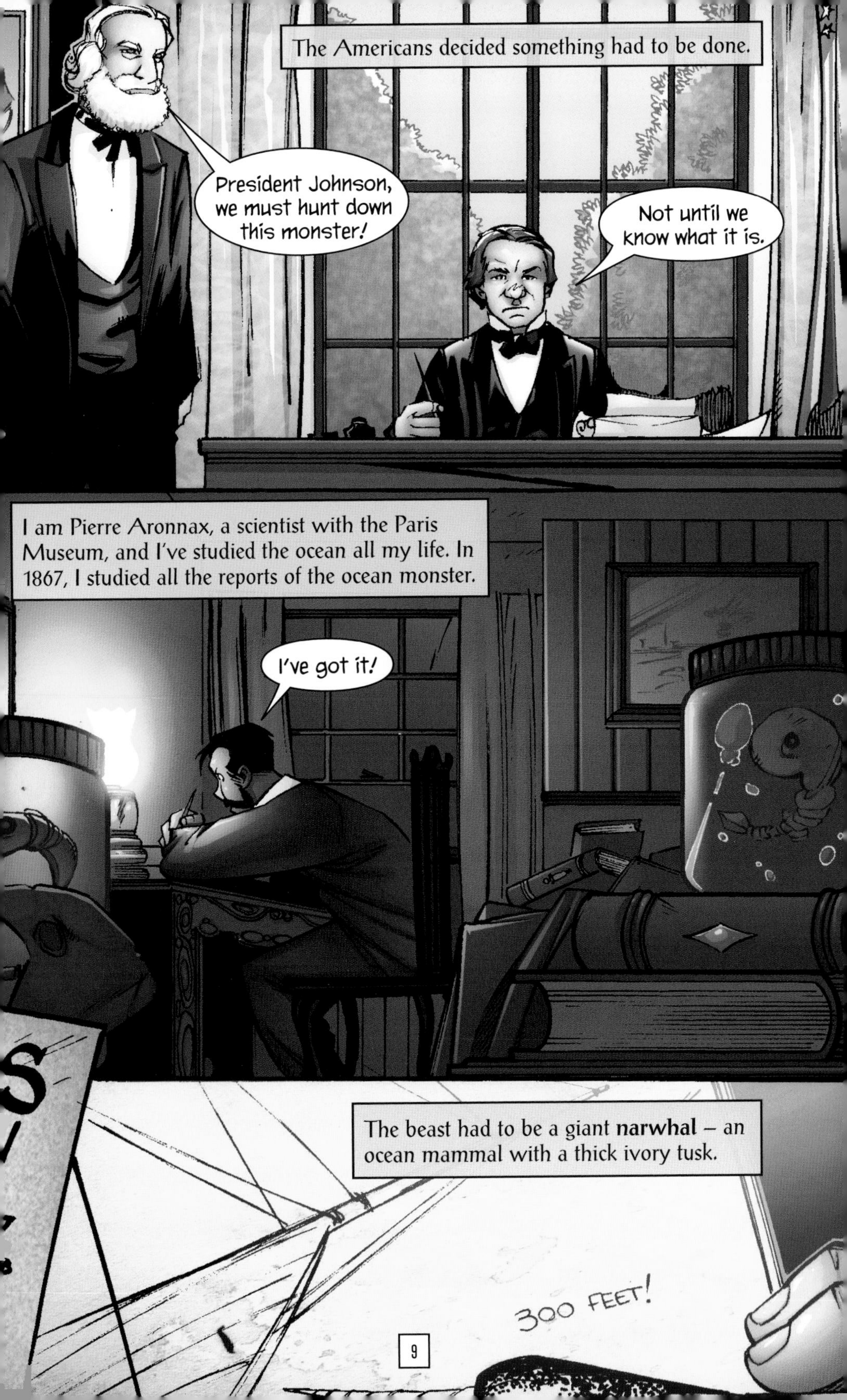
The Americans decided something had to be done.
President Johnson, we must hunt down this monster!
Not until we know what it is.
I am Pierre Aronnax, a scientist with the Paris Museum, and I've studied the ocean all my life. In 1867, I studied all the reports of the ocean monster.
I've got it!
The beast had to be a giant **narwhal** – an ocean mammal with a thick ivory tusk.
300 FEET!

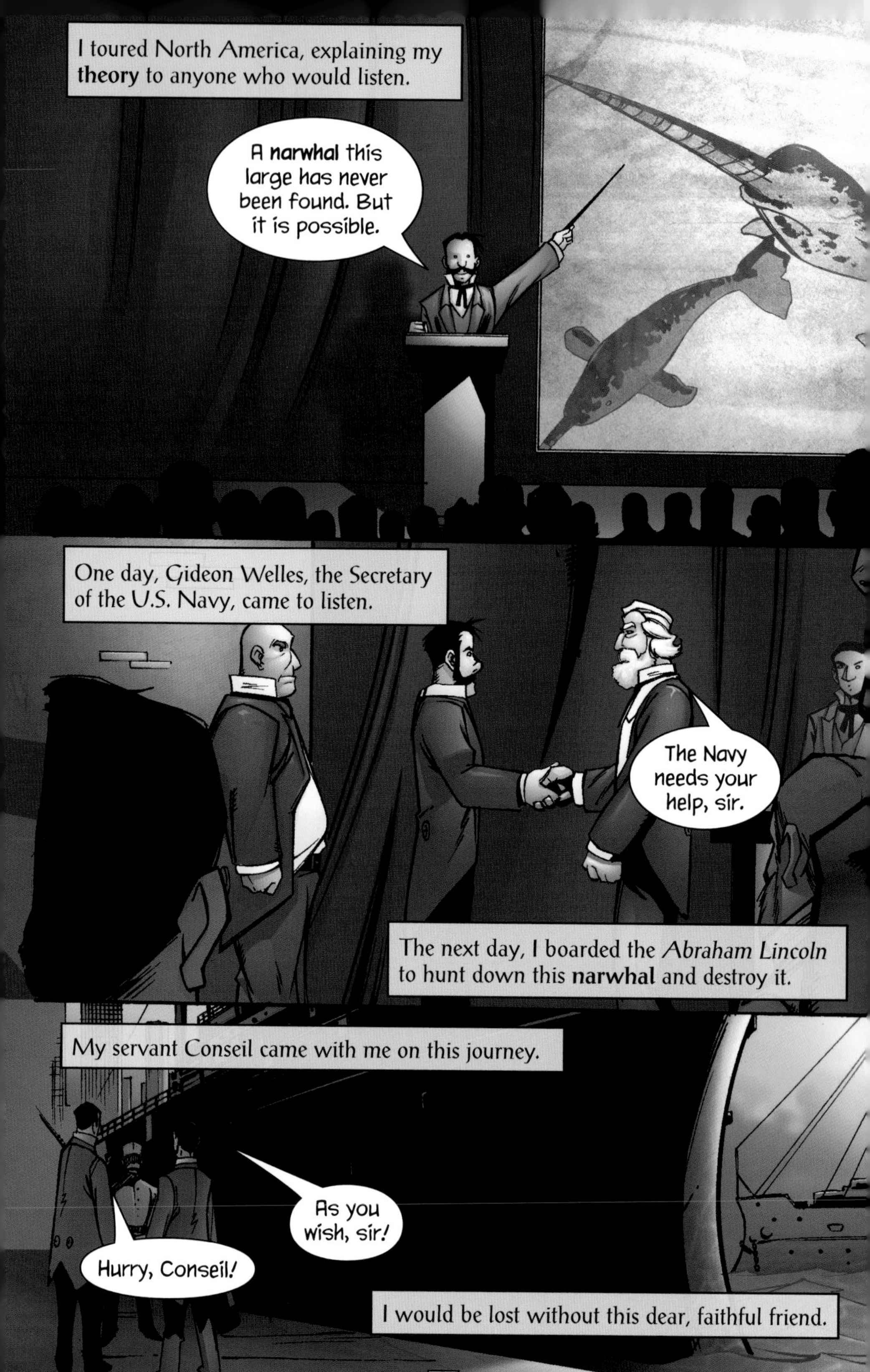
I toured North America, explaining my **theory** to anyone who would listen.
A **narwhal** this large has never been found. But it is possible.
One day, Gideon Welles, the Secretary of the U.S. Navy, came to listen.
The Navy needs your help, sir.
The next day, I boarded the *Abraham Lincoln* to hunt down this **narwhal** and destroy it.
My servant Conseil came with me on this journey.
Hurry, Conseil!
As you wish, sir!
I would be lost without this dear, faithful friend.

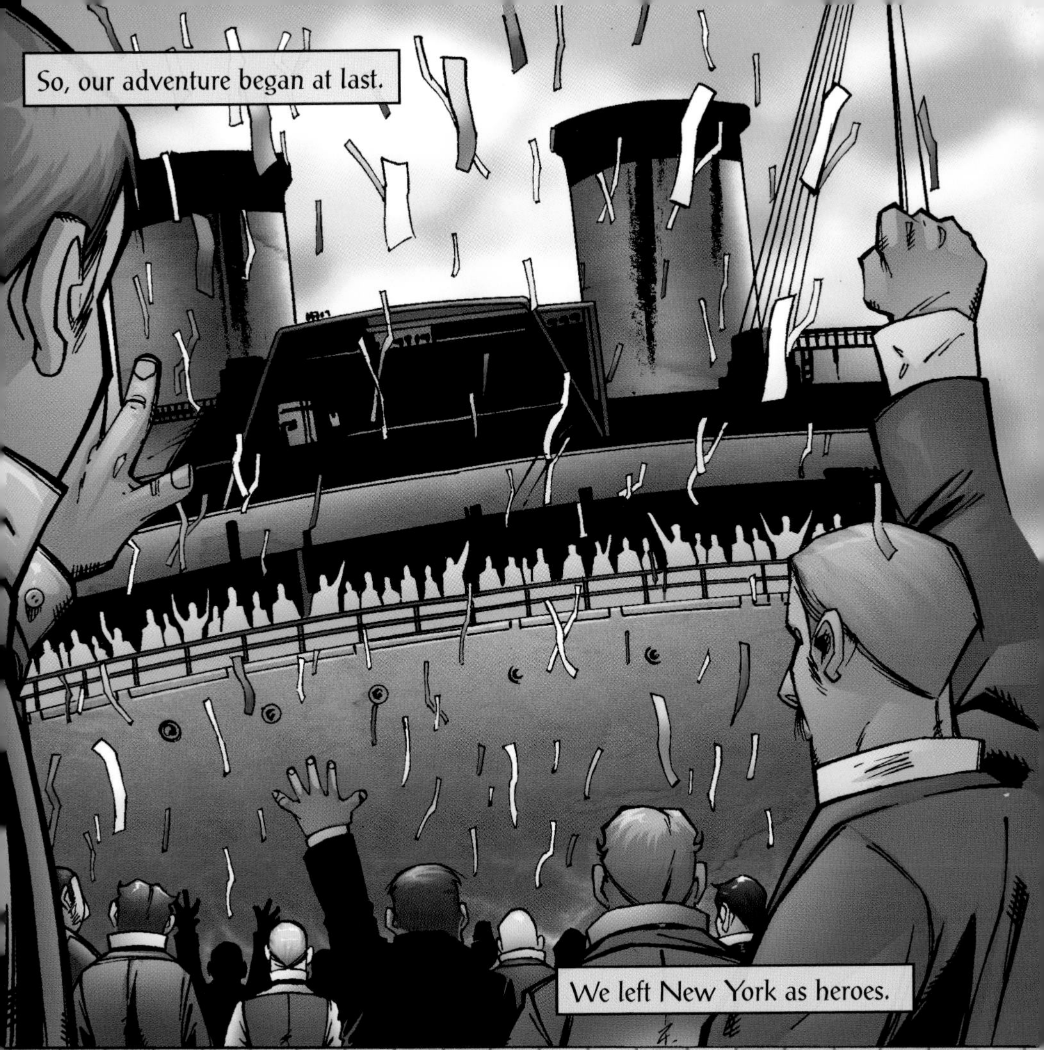
So, our adventure began at last.
We left New York as heroes.

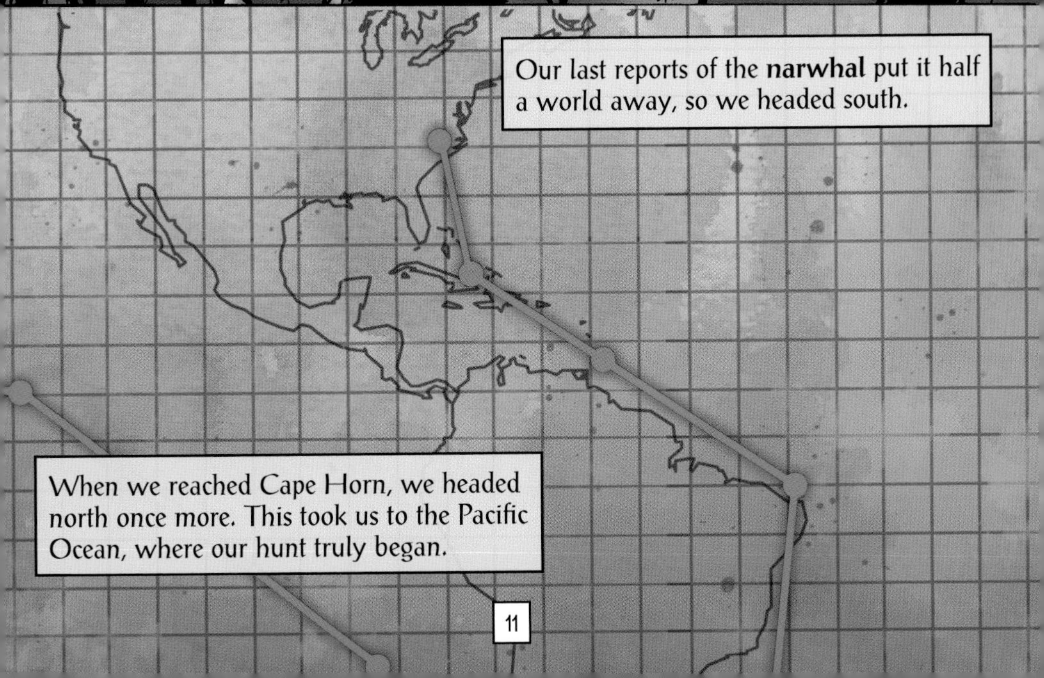
Our last reports of the **narwhal** put it half a world away, so we headed south.
When we reached Cape Horn, we headed north once more. This took us to the Pacific Ocean, where our hunt truly began.

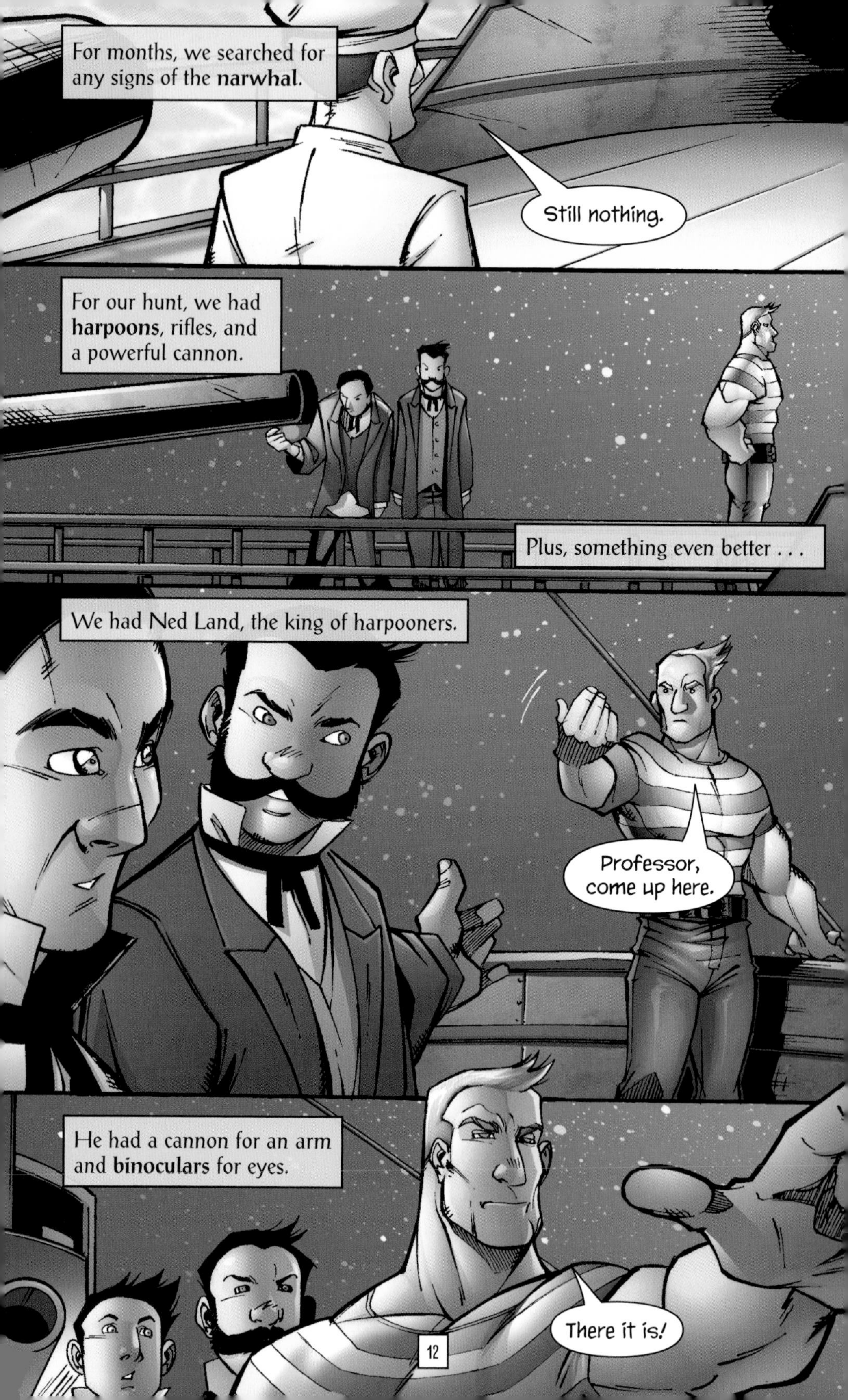
For months, we searched for any signs of the **narwhal**.
Still nothing.
For our hunt, we had **harpoons**, rifles, and a powerful cannon.
Plus, something even better . . .
We had Ned Land, the king of harpooners.
Professor, come up here.
He had a cannon for an arm and **binoculars** for eyes.
There it is!

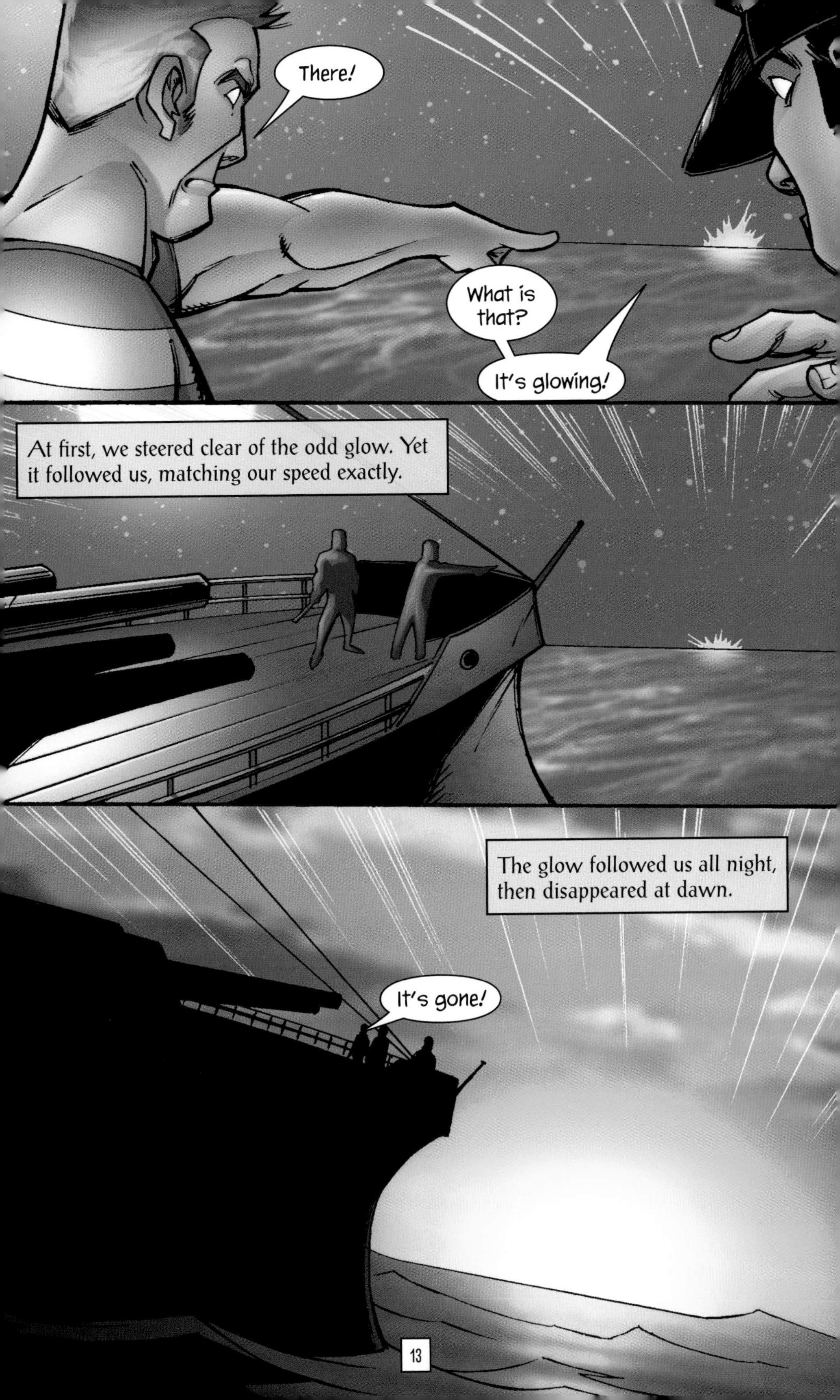
There!
What is that?
It's glowing!
At first, we steered clear of the odd glow. Yet it followed us, matching our speed exactly.
The glow followed us all night, then disappeared at dawn.
It's gone!

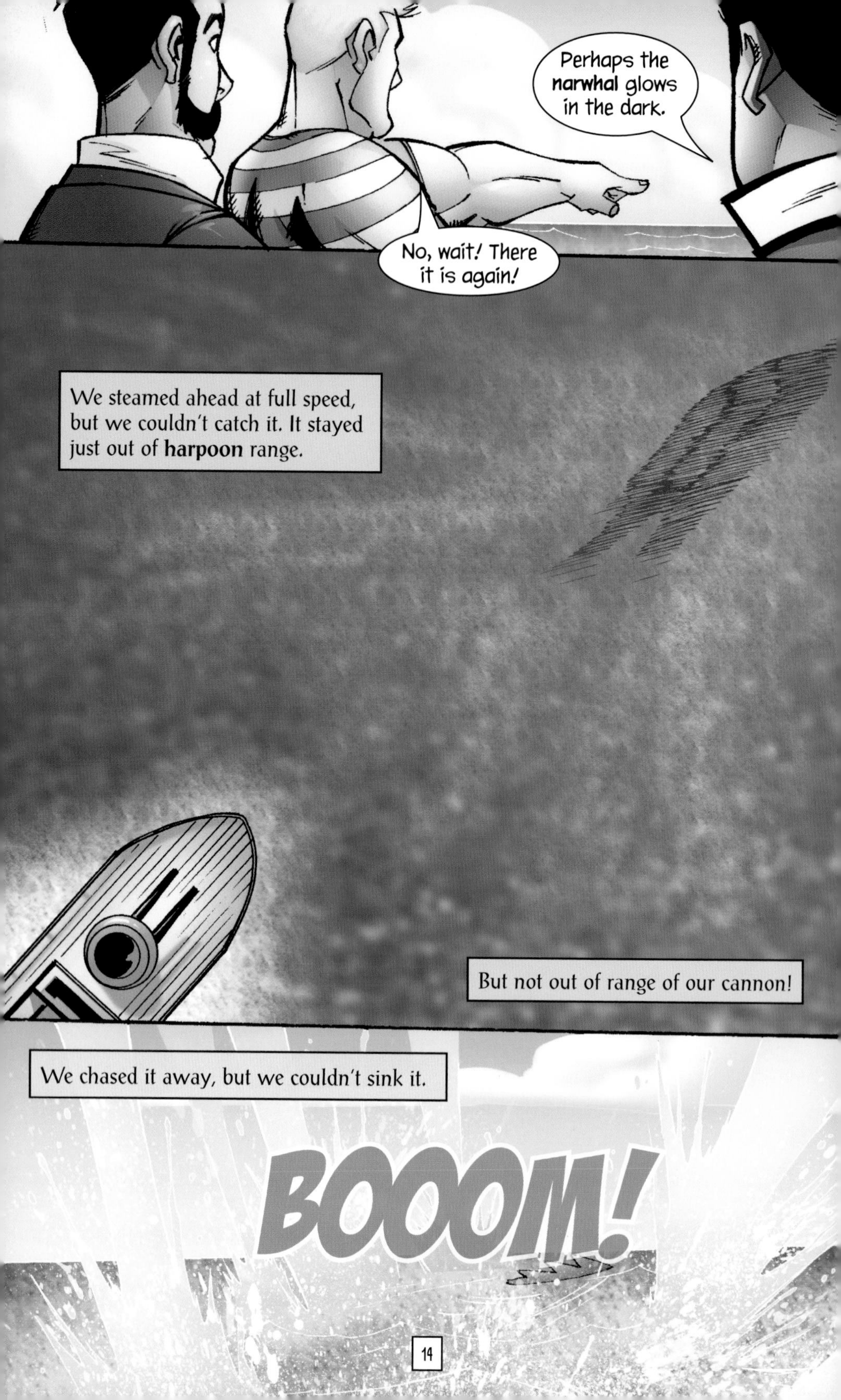

Perhaps the **narwhal** glows in the dark.

No, wait! There it is again!

We steamed ahead at full speed, but we couldn't catch it. It stayed just out of **harpoon** range.

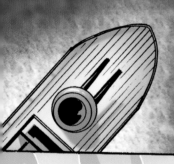

But not out of range of our cannon!

We chased it away, but we couldn't sink it.

BOOOM!

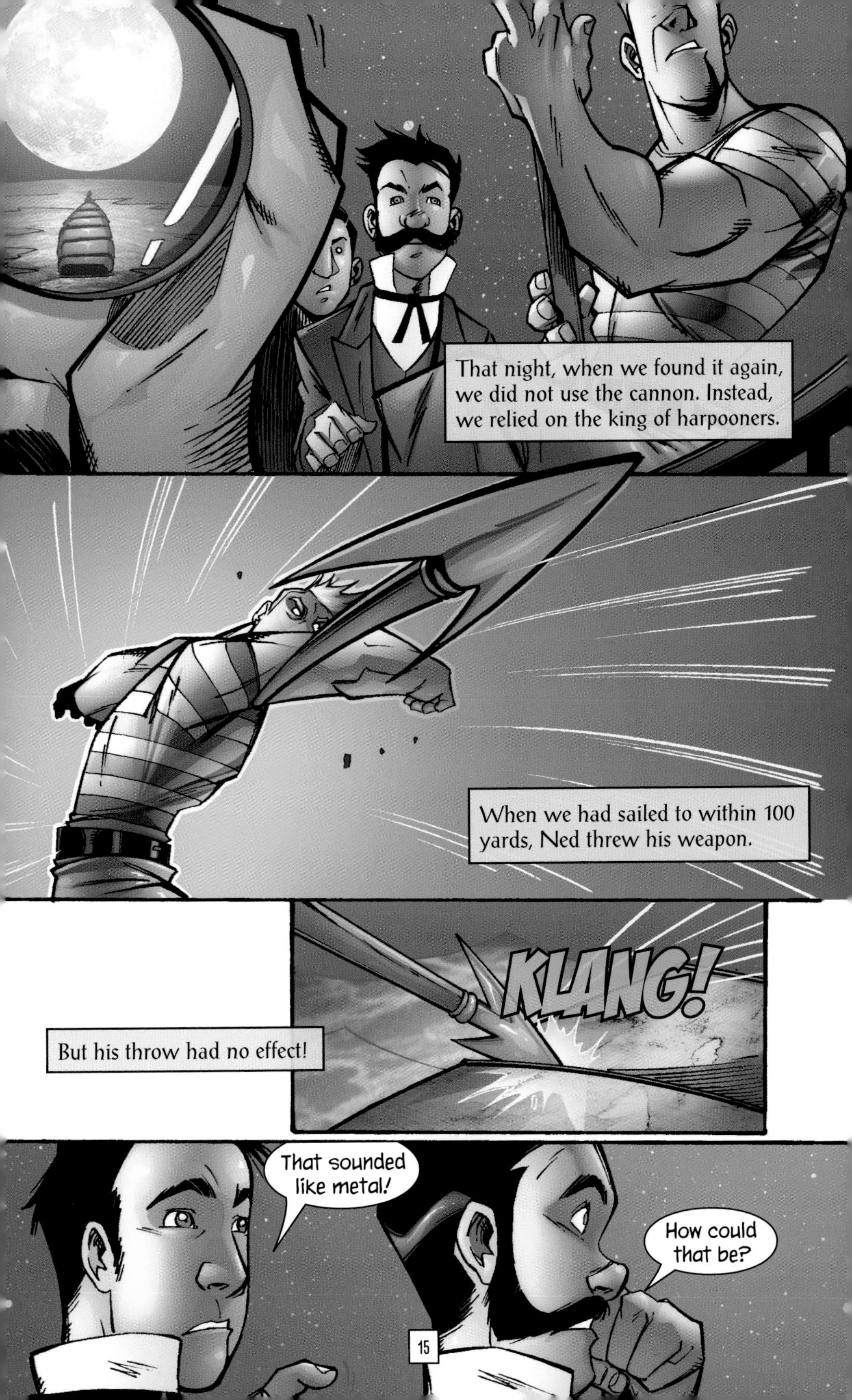
That night, when we found it again, we did not use the cannon. Instead, we relied on the king of harpooners.
When we had sailed to within 100 yards, Ned threw his weapon.
But his throw had no effect!
KLANG!
That sounded like metal!
How could that be?

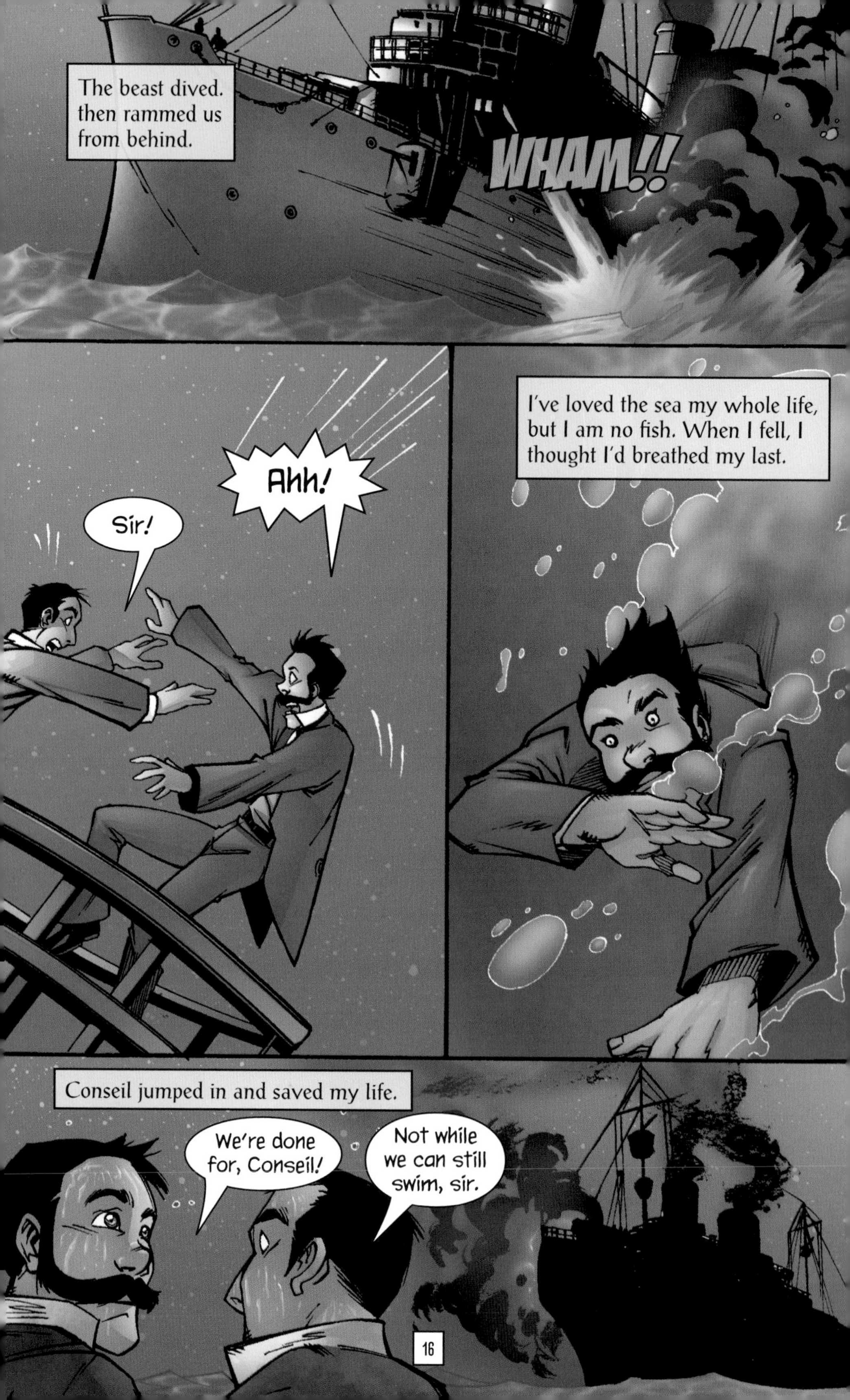
The beast dived. then rammed us from behind.
WHAM!!
Sir!
Ahh!
I've loved the sea my whole life, but I am no fish. When I fell, I thought I'd breathed my last.
Conseil jumped in and saved my life.
We're done for, Conseil!
Not while we can still swim, sir.

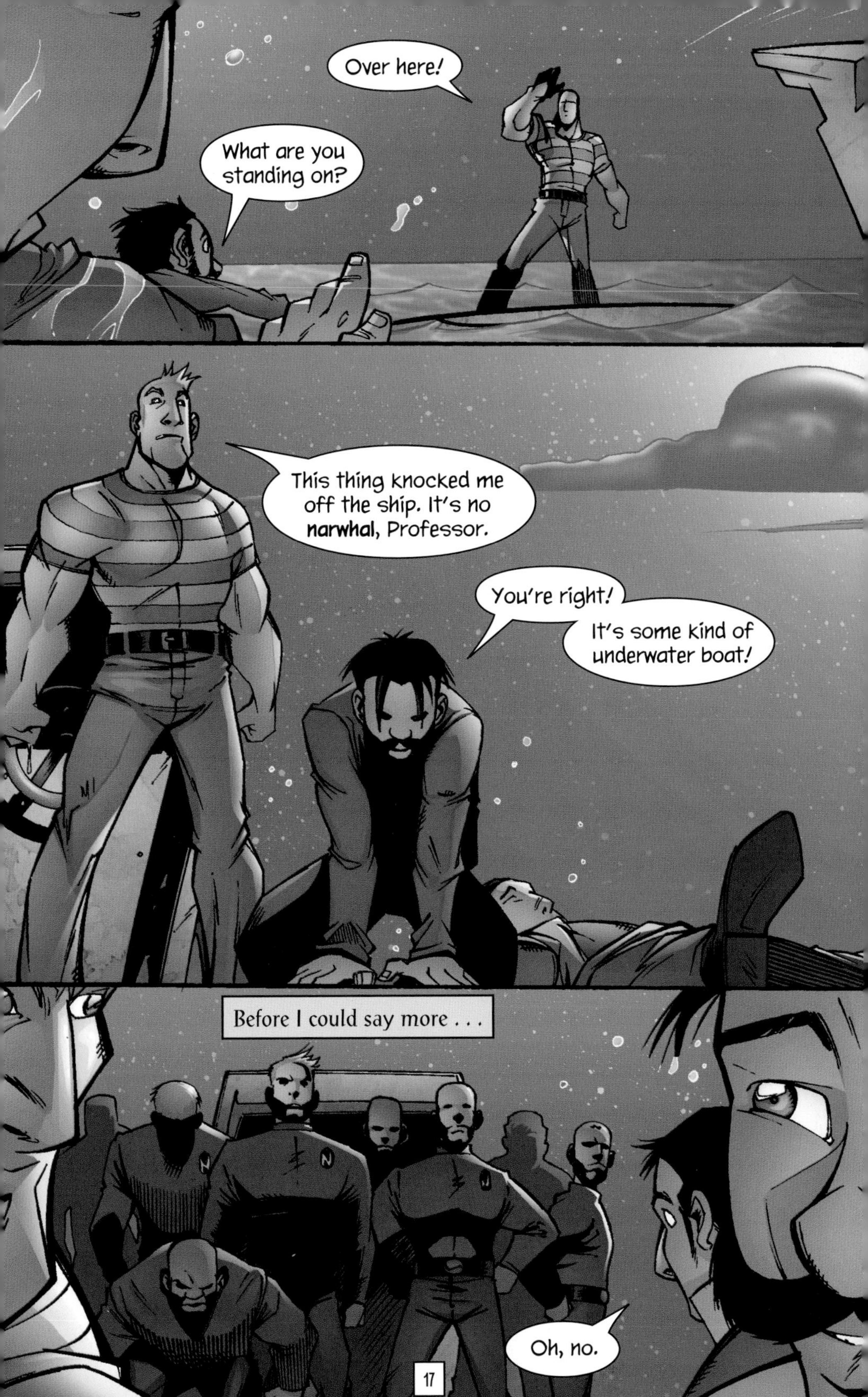
Over here!
What are you standing on?
This thing knocked me off the ship. It's no **narwhal**, Professor.
You're right!
It's some kind of underwater boat!
Before I could say more . . .
Oh, no.

CHAPTER 2

INSIDE THE *NAUTILUS*

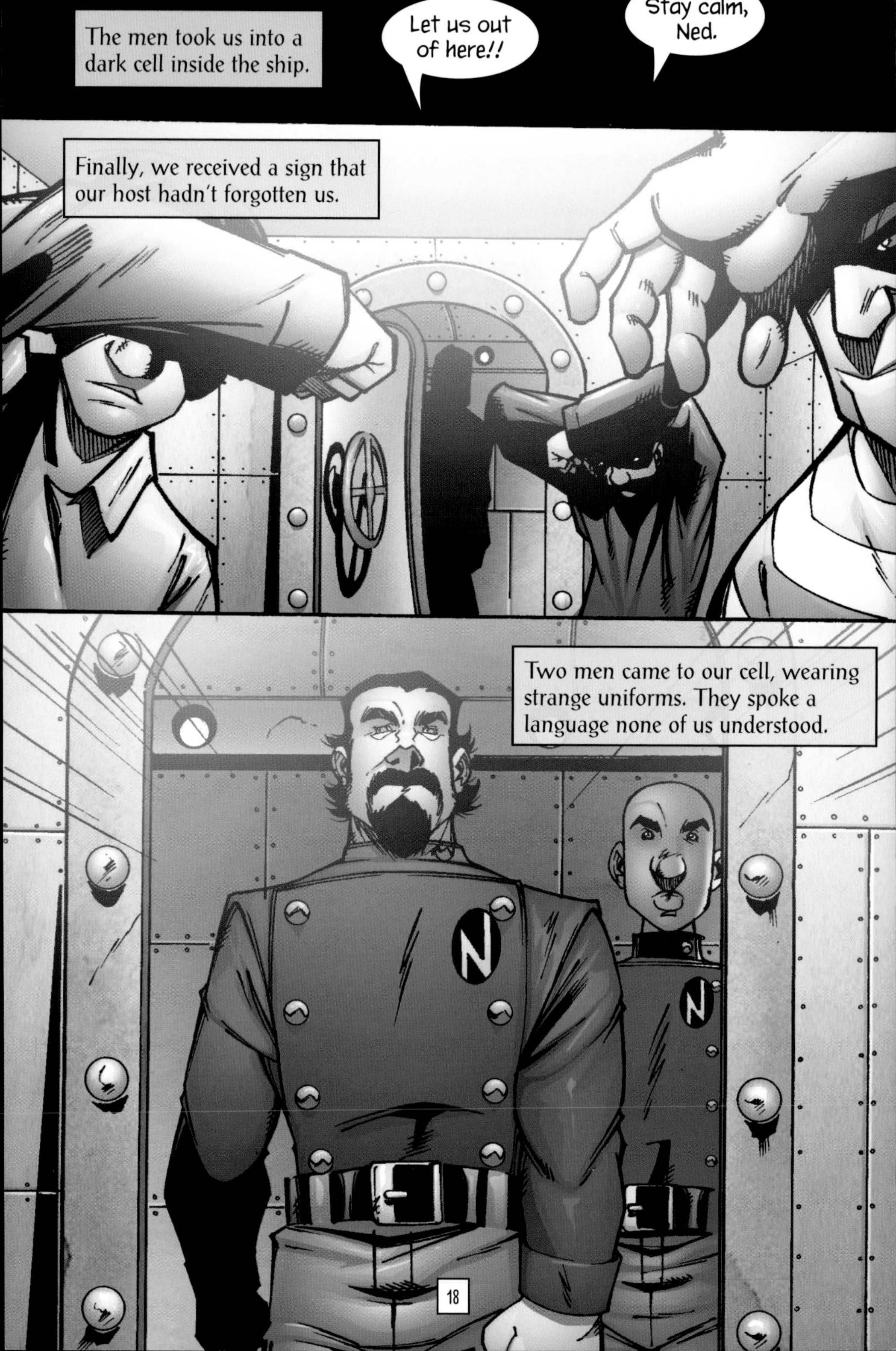
The men took us into a dark cell inside the ship.
Let us out of here!!
Stay calm, Ned.
Finally, we received a sign that our host hadn't forgotten us.
Two men came to our cell, wearing strange uniforms. They spoke a language none of us understood.

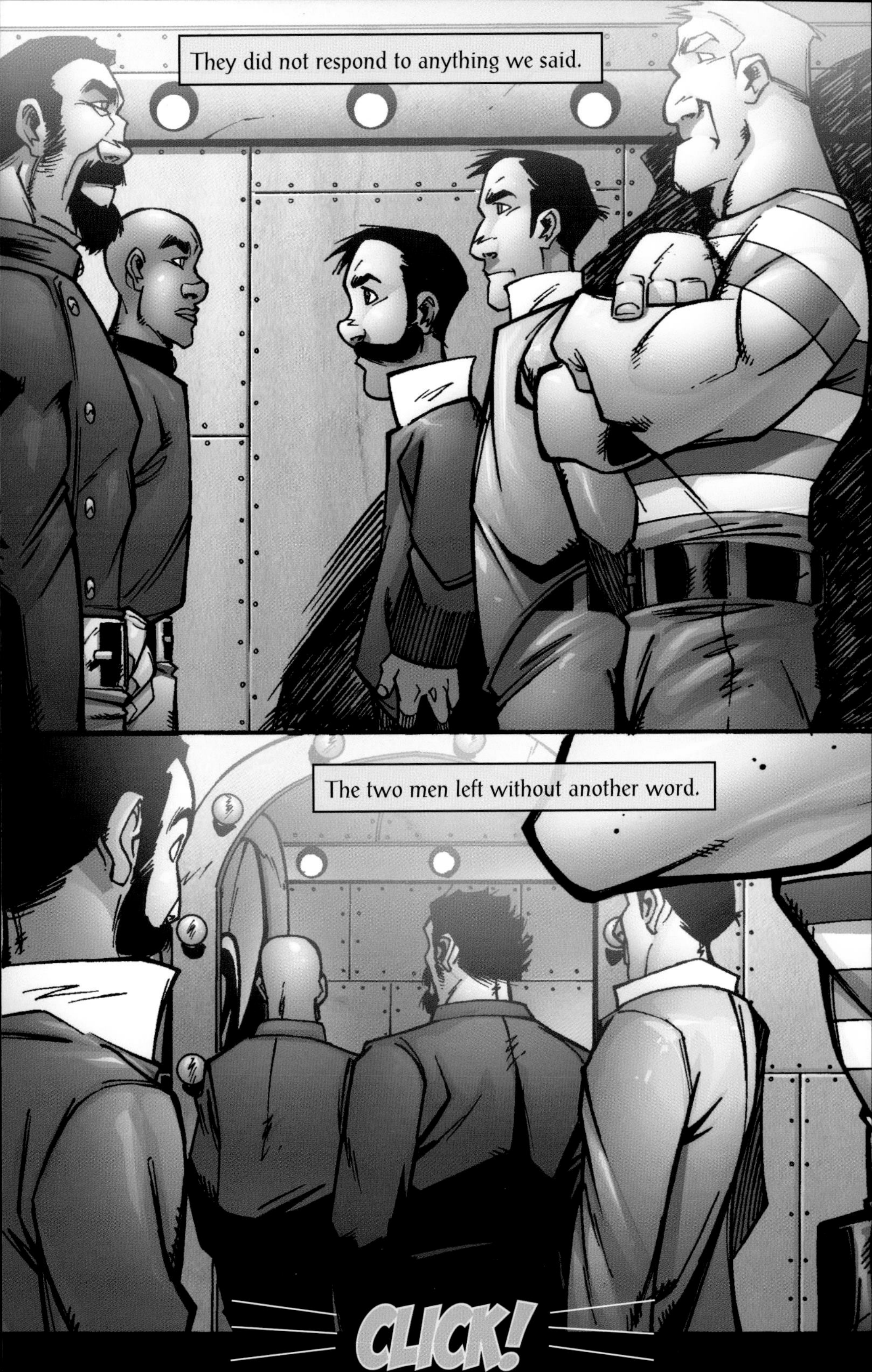
They did not respond to anything we said.
The two men left without another word.
CLICK!

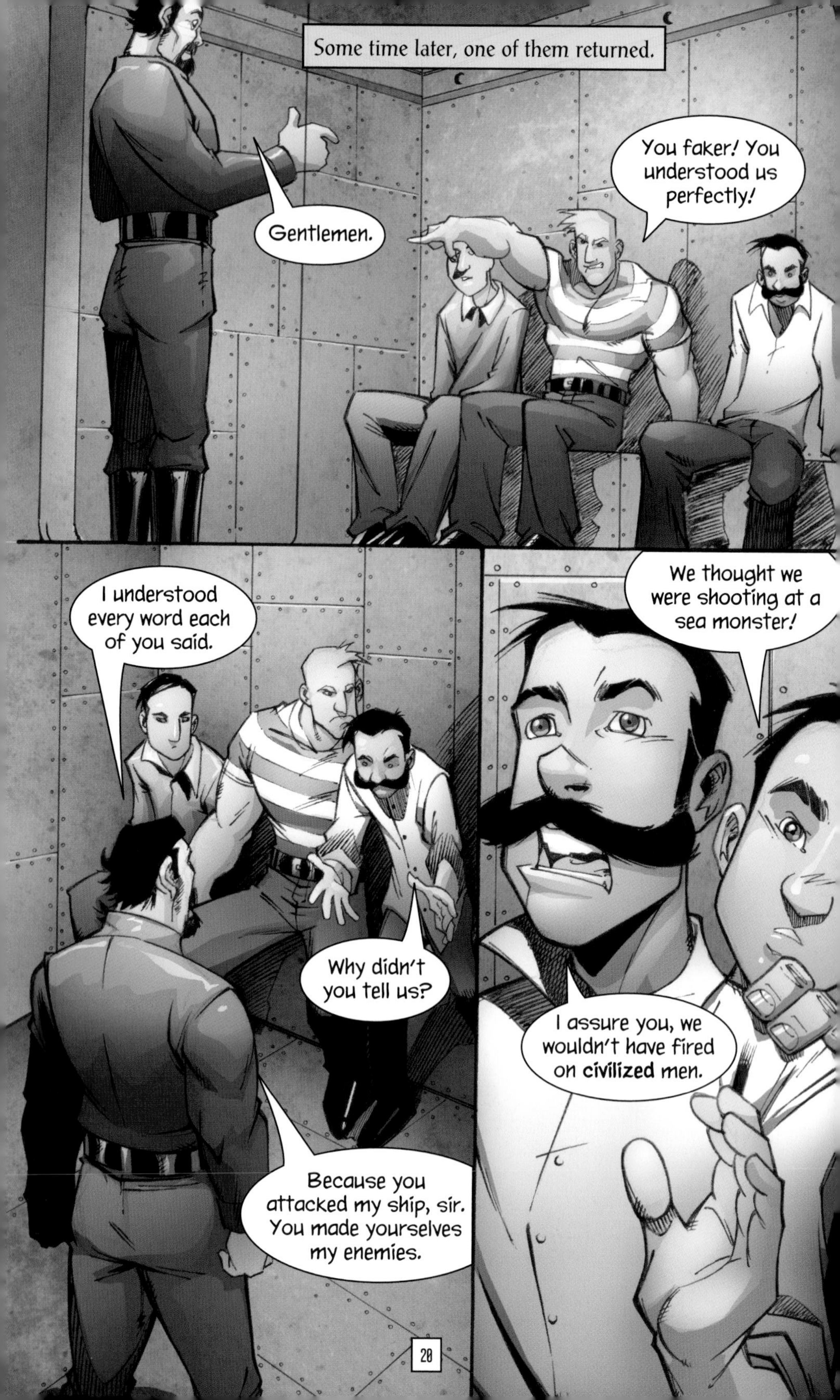
Some time later, one of them returned.
Gentlemen.
You faker! You understood us perfectly!
I understood every word each of you said.
Why didn't you tell us?
Because you attacked my ship, sir. You made yourselves my enemies.
We thought we were shooting at a sea monster!
I assure you, we wouldn't have fired on **civilized** men.

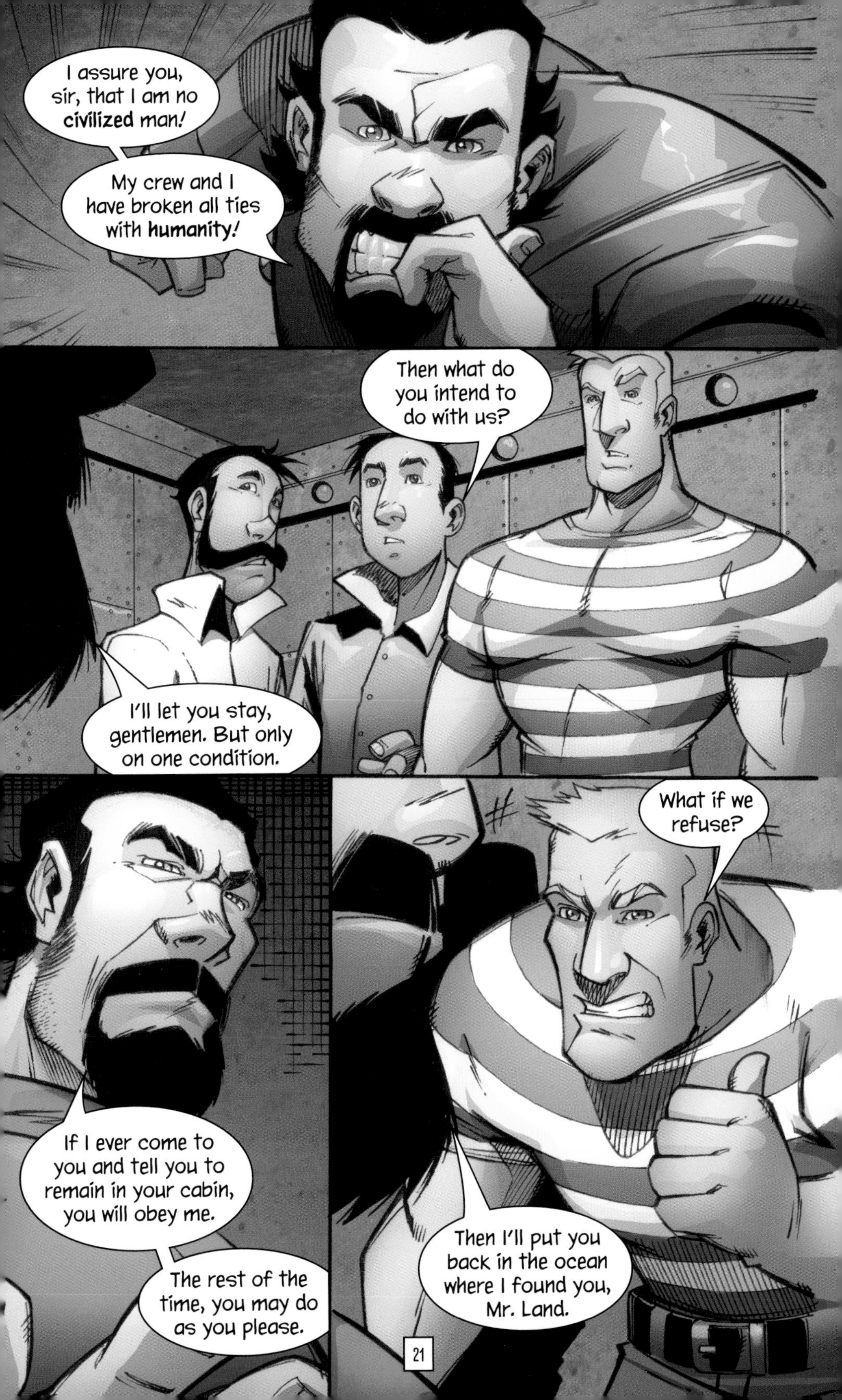
I assure you, sir, that I am no **civilized** man!
My crew and I have broken all ties with **humanity**!
Then what do you intend to do with us?
I'll let you stay, gentlemen. But only on one condition.
If I ever come to you and tell you to remain in your cabin, you will obey me.
The rest of the time, you may do as you please.
What if we refuse?
Then I'll put you back in the ocean where I found you, Mr. Land.

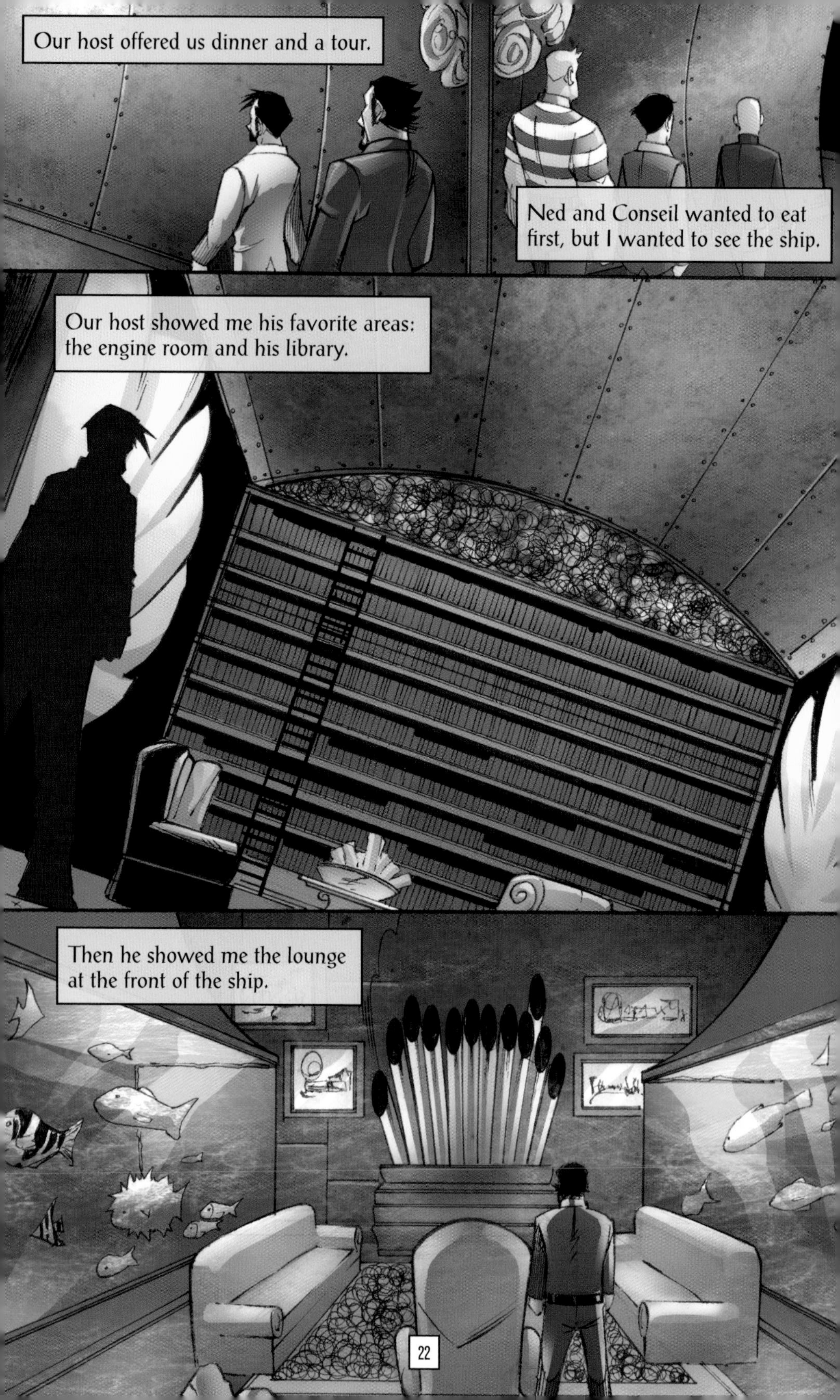
Our host offered us dinner and a tour.
Ned and Conseil wanted to eat first, but I wanted to see the ship.
Our host showed me his favorite areas: the engine room and his library.
Then he showed me the lounge at the front of the ship.

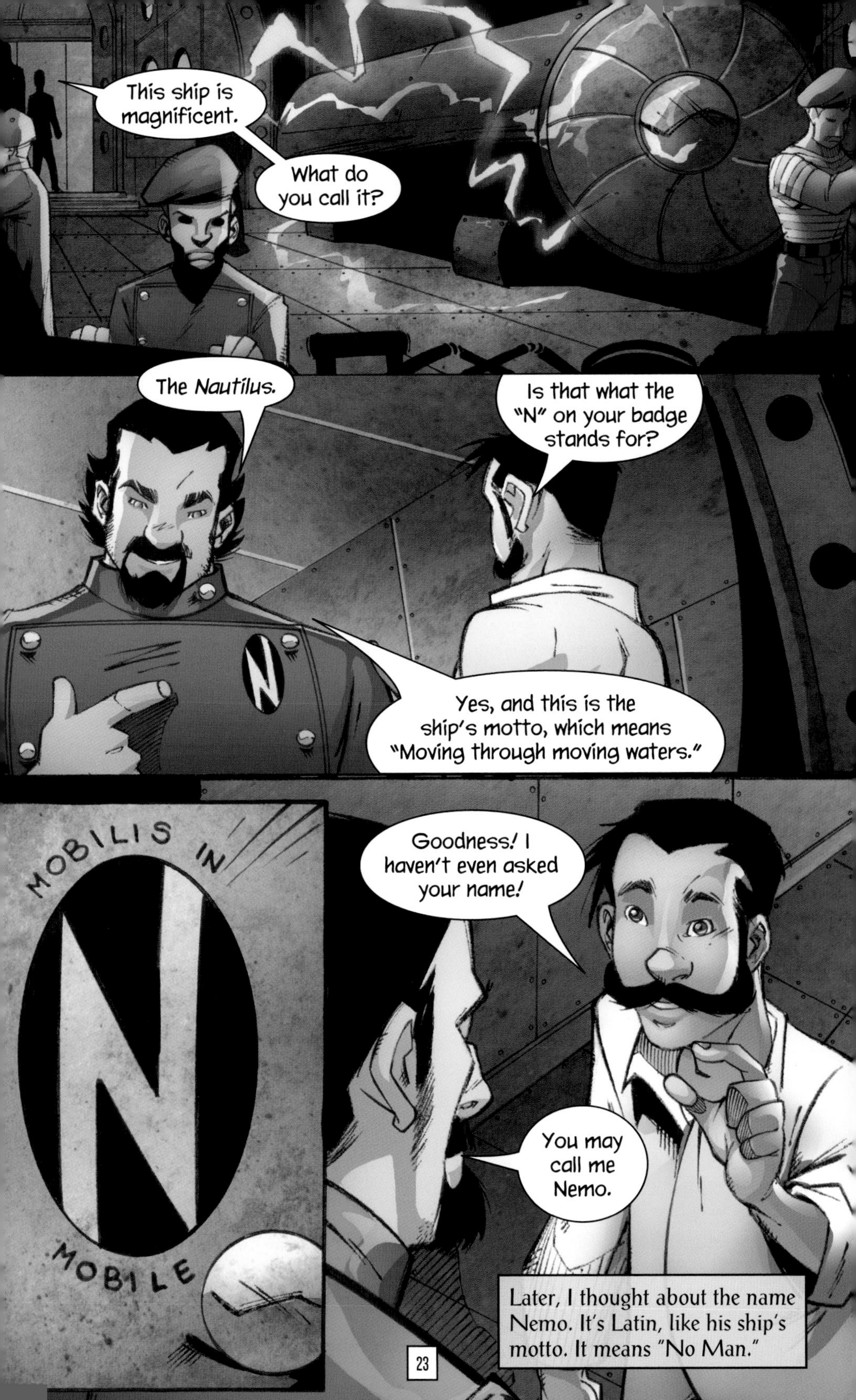
This ship is magnificent.
What do you call it?
The *Nautilus*.
Is that what the "N" on your badge stands for?
Yes, and this is the ship's motto, which means "Moving through moving waters."
MOBILIS IN
N
MOBILE
Goodness! I haven't even asked your name!
You may call me Nemo.
Later, I thought about the name Nemo. It's Latin, like his ship's motto. It means "No Man."

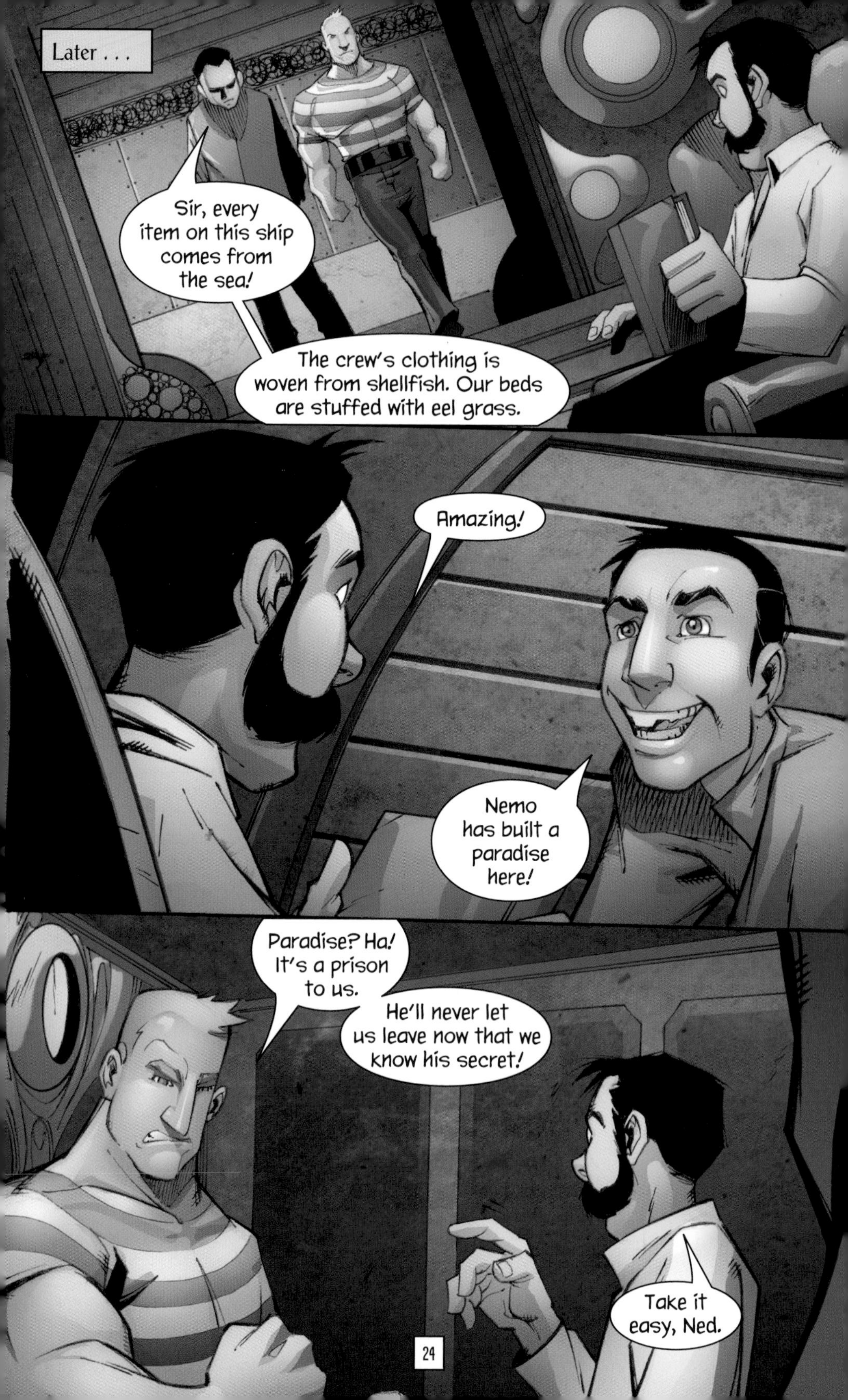
Later . . .
Sir, every item on this ship comes from the sea!
The crew's clothing is woven from shellfish. Our beds are stuffed with eel grass.
Amazing!
Nemo has built a paradise here!
Paradise? Ha! It's a prison to us.
He'll never let us leave now that we know his secret!
Take it easy, Ned.

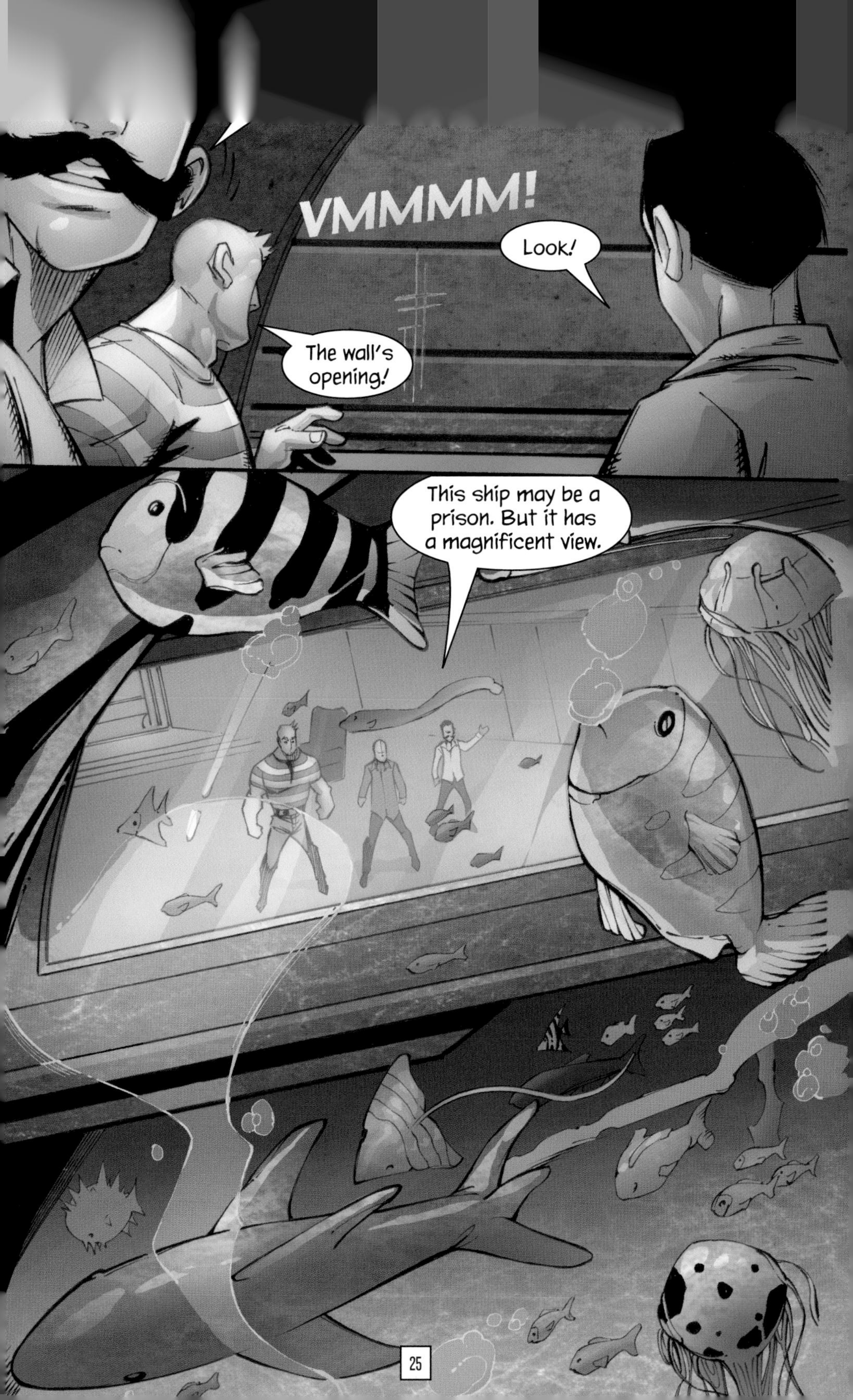
VMMMM!
Look!
The wall's opening!
This ship may be a prison. But it has a magnificent view.

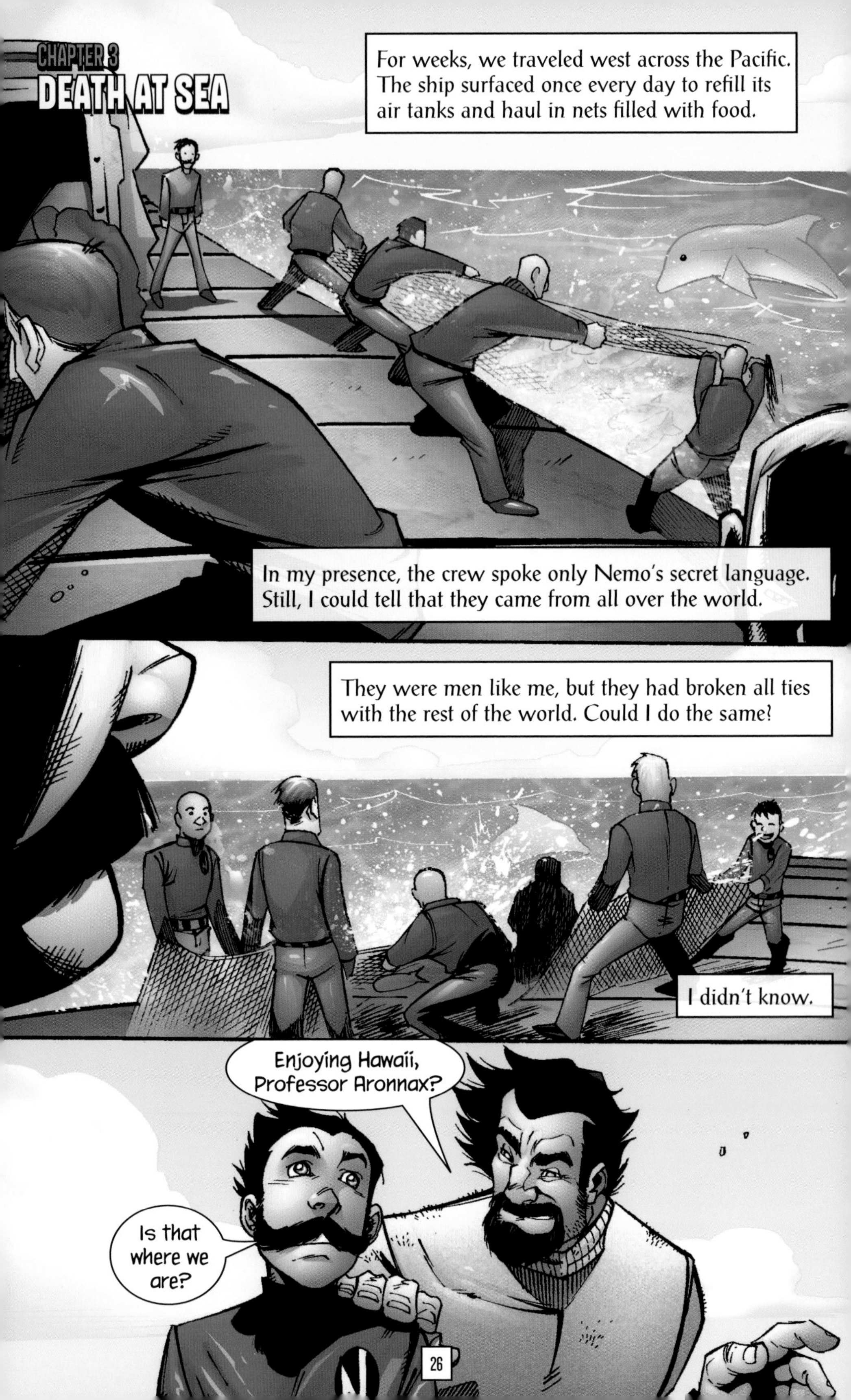
CHAPTER 3
DEATH AT SEA
For weeks, we traveled west across the Pacific. The ship surfaced once every day to refill its air tanks and haul in nets filled with food.
In my presence, the crew spoke only Nemo's secret language. Still, I could tell that they came from all over the world.
They were men like me, but they had broken all ties with the rest of the world. Could I do the same?
I didn't know.
Enjoying Hawaii, Professor Aronnax?
Is that where we are?

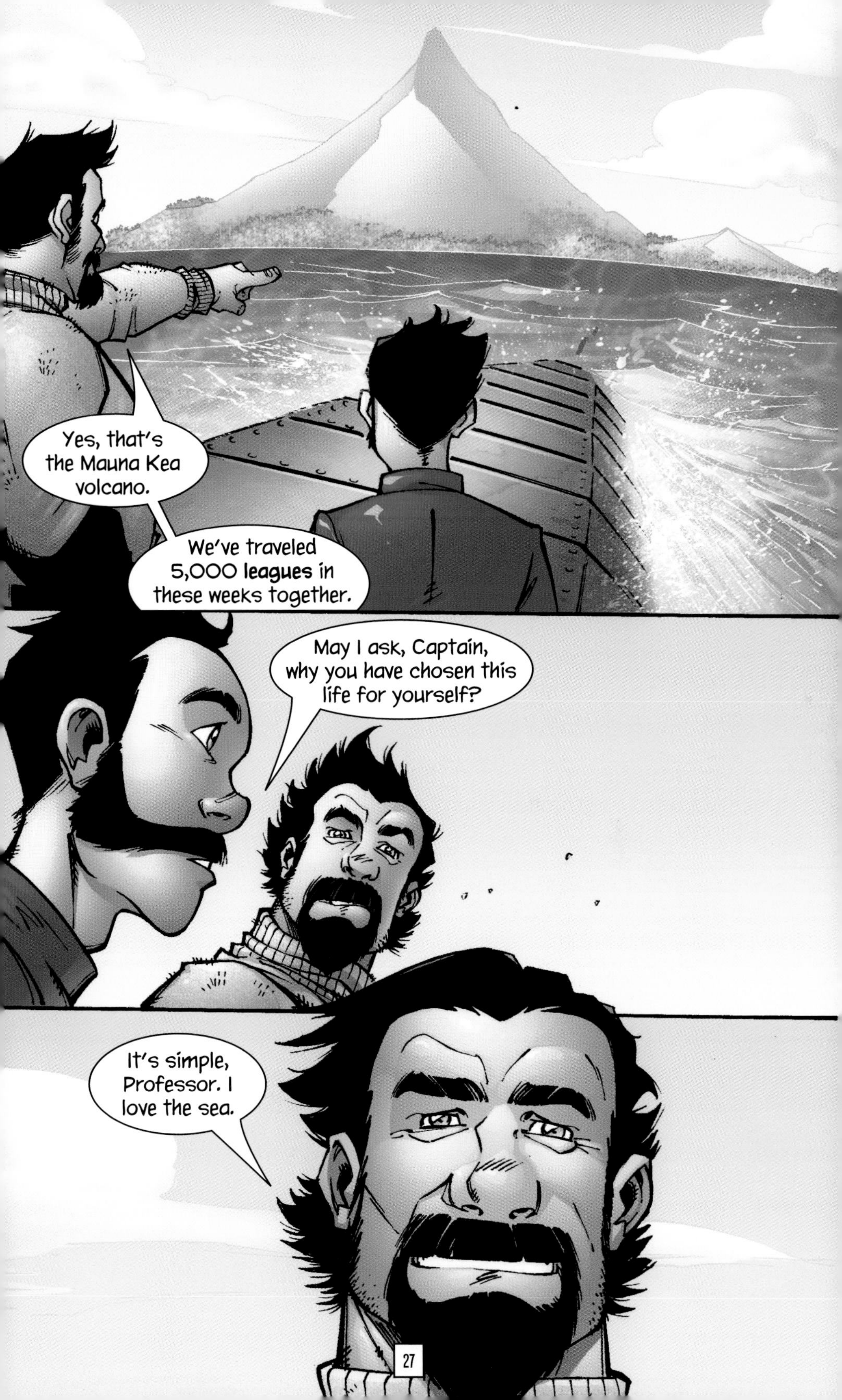

Yes, that's the Mauna Kea volcano.
We've traveled 5,000 **leagues** in these weeks together.
May I ask, Captain, why you have chosen this life for yourself?
It's simple, Professor. I love the sea.

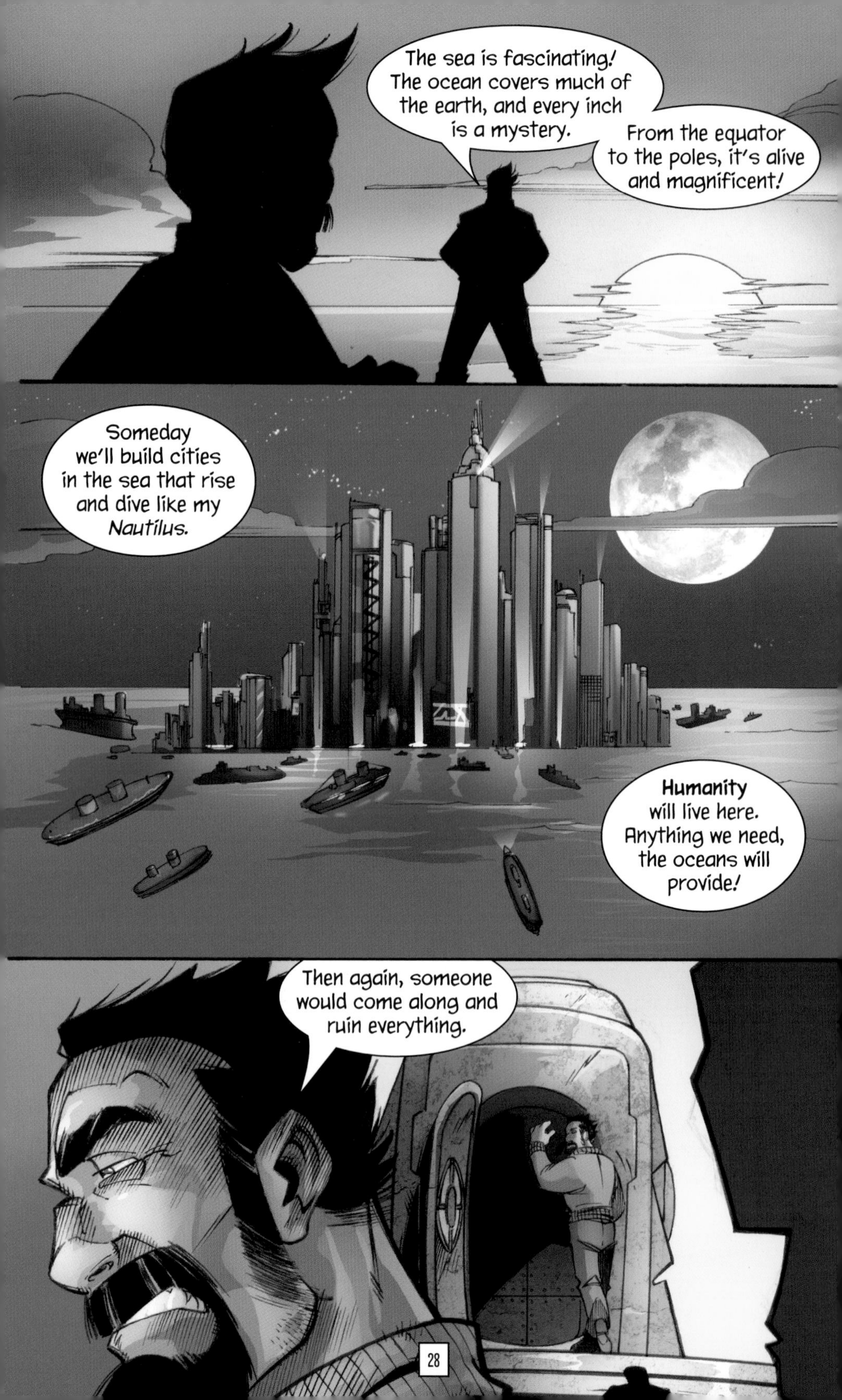
The sea is fascinating! The ocean covers much of the earth, and every inch is a mystery.
From the equator to the poles, it's alive and magnificent!
Someday we'll build cities in the sea that rise and dive like my *Nautilus*.
Humanity will live here. Anything we need, the oceans will provide!
Then again, someone would come along and ruin everything.

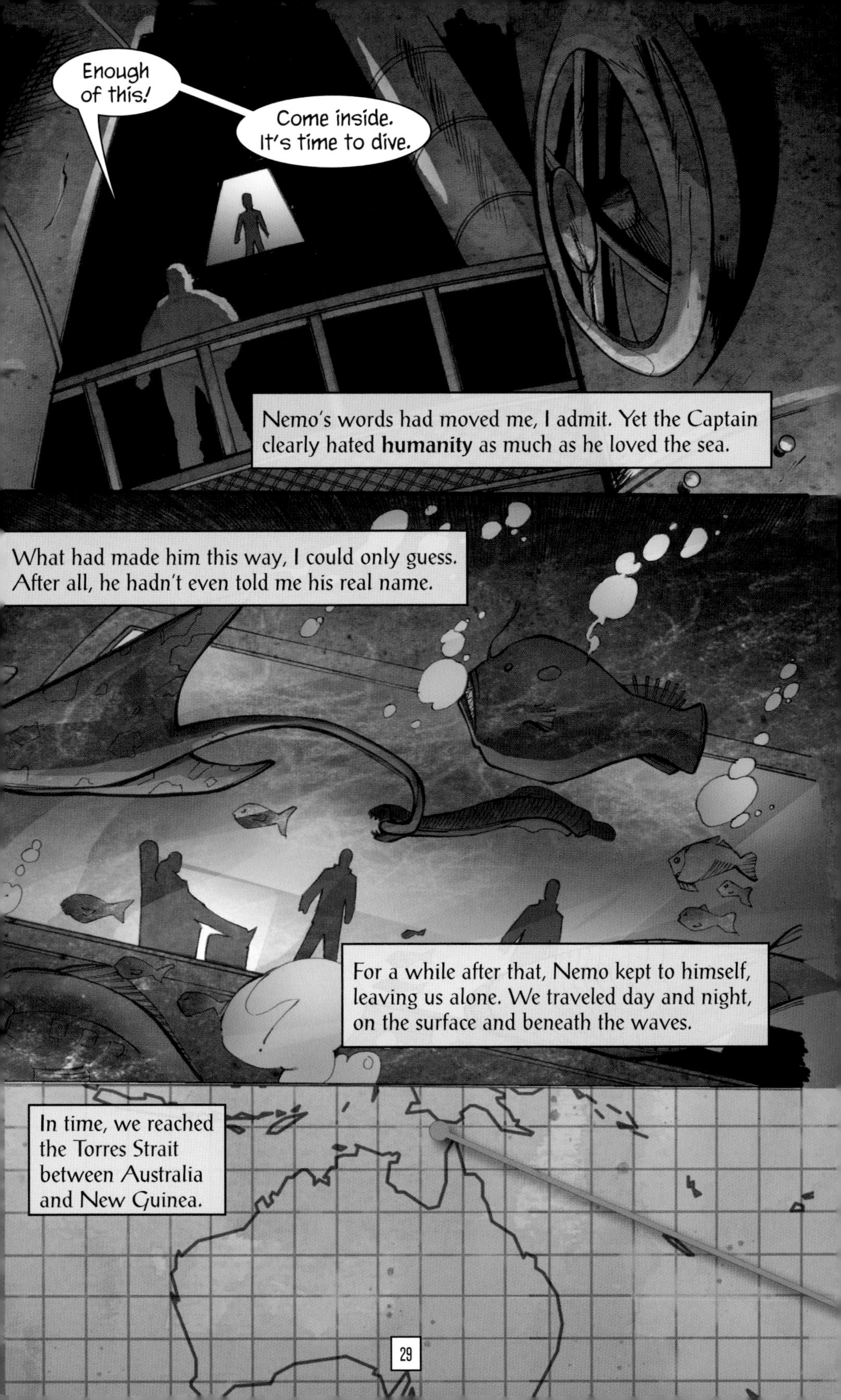
Enough of this!
Come inside. It's time to dive.
Nemo's words had moved me, I admit. Yet the Captain clearly hated **humanity** as much as he loved the sea.
What had made him this way, I could only guess. After all, he hadn't even told me his real name.
For a while after that, Nemo kept to himself, leaving us alone. We traveled day and night, on the surface and beneath the waves.
In time, we reached the Torres Strait between Australia and New Guinea.

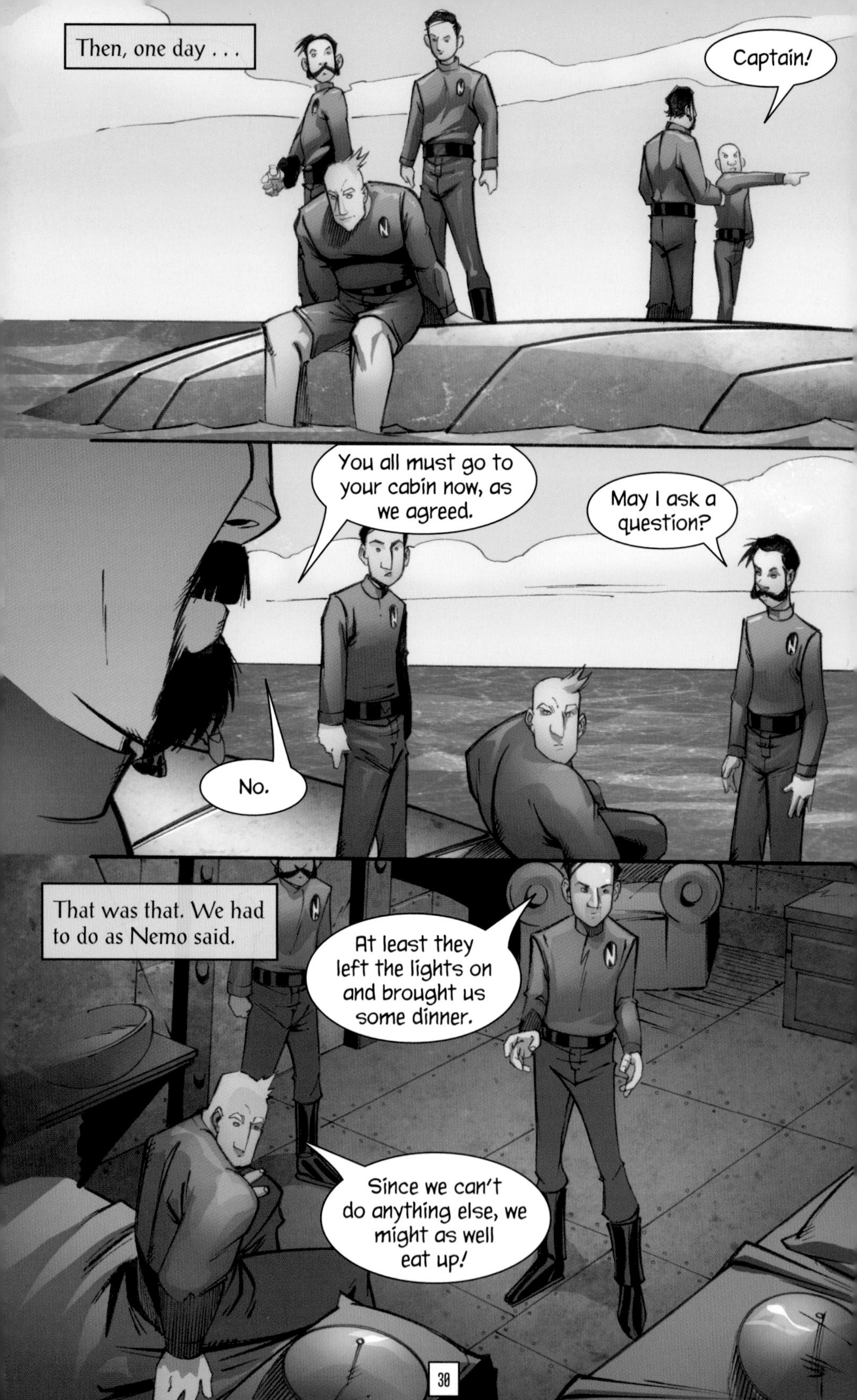
Then, one day . . .
Captain!
You all must go to your cabin now, as we agreed.
May I ask a question?
No.
That was that. We had to do as Nemo said.
At least they left the lights on and brought us some dinner.
Since we can't do anything else, we might as well eat up!

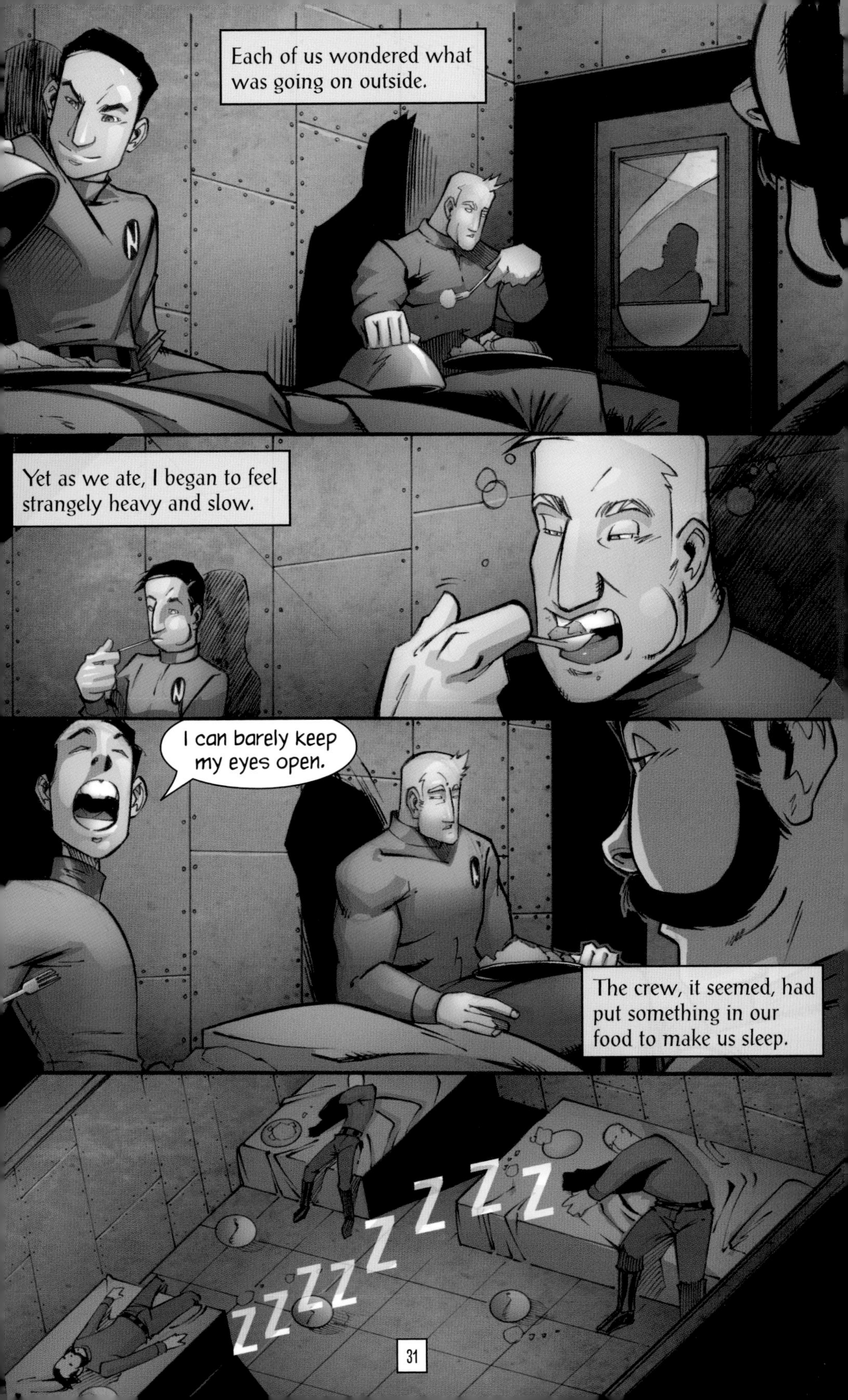

Each of us wondered what was going on outside.
Yet as we ate, I began to feel strangely heavy and slow.
I can barely keep my eyes open.
The crew, it seemed, had put something in our food to make us sleep.
ZZZZZ
ZZZZZ

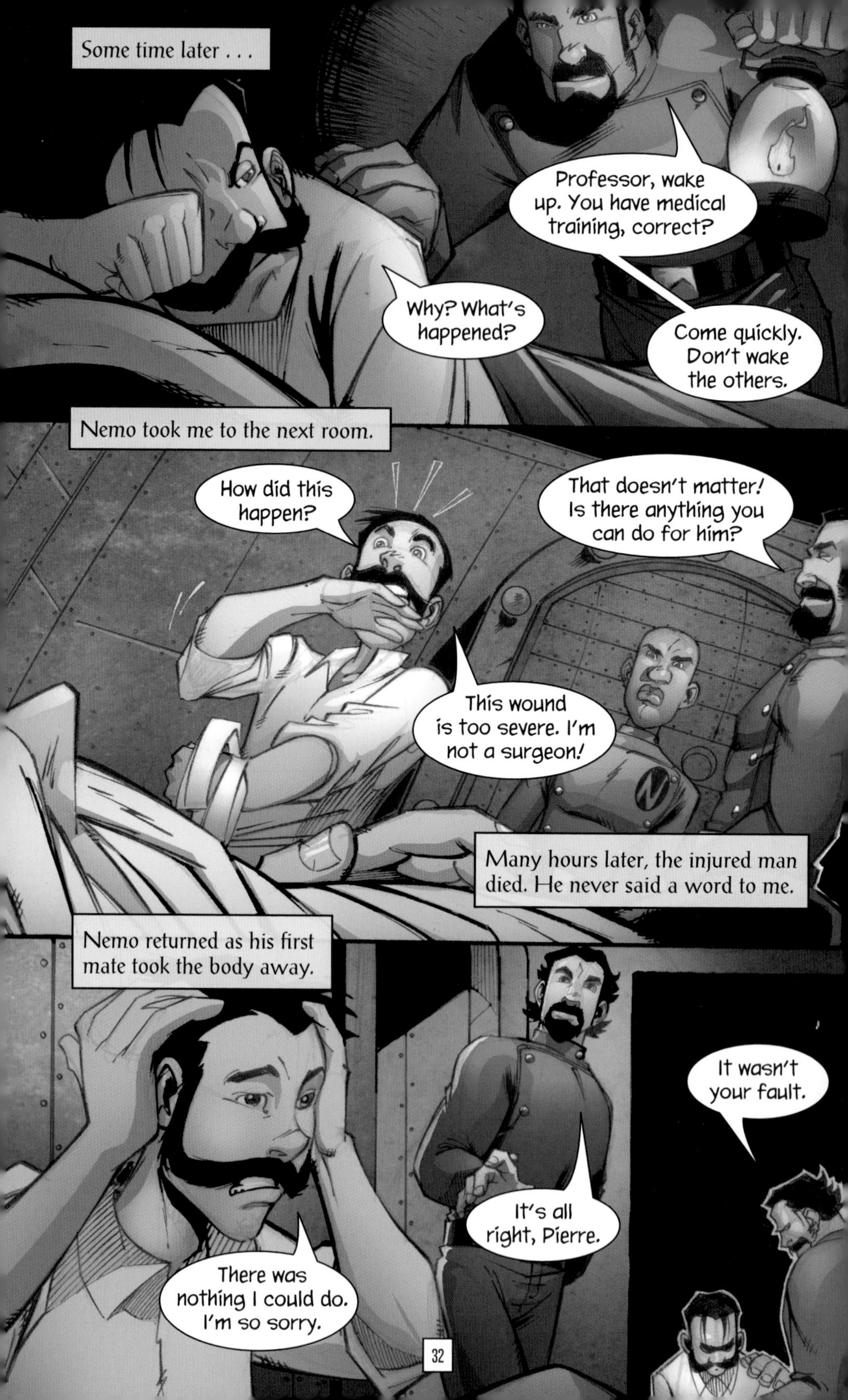
Some time later . . .
Professor, wake up. You have medical training, correct?
Why? What's happened?
Come quickly. Don't wake the others.
Nemo took me to the next room.
How did this happen?
That doesn't matter! Is there anything you can do for him?
This wound is too severe. I'm not a surgeon!
Many hours later, the injured man died. He never said a word to me.
Nemo returned as his first mate took the body away.
It wasn't your fault.
It's all right, Pierre.
There was nothing I could do. I'm so sorry.

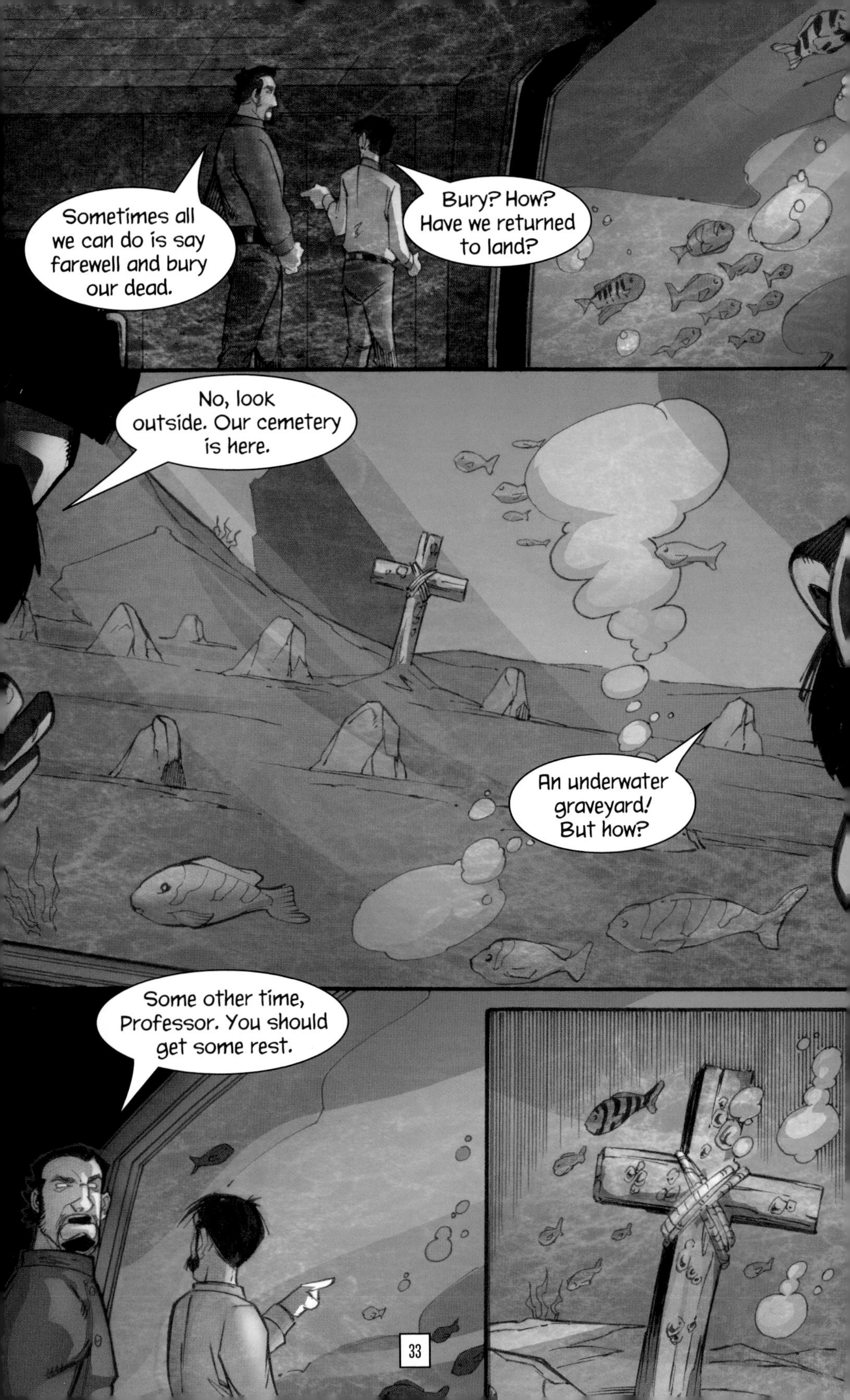
Sometimes all we can do is say farewell and bury our dead.
Bury? How? Have we returned to land?
No, look outside. Our cemetery is here.
An underwater graveyard! But how?
Some other time, Professor. You should get some rest.

CHAPTER 4
UNDERWATER ADVENTURES

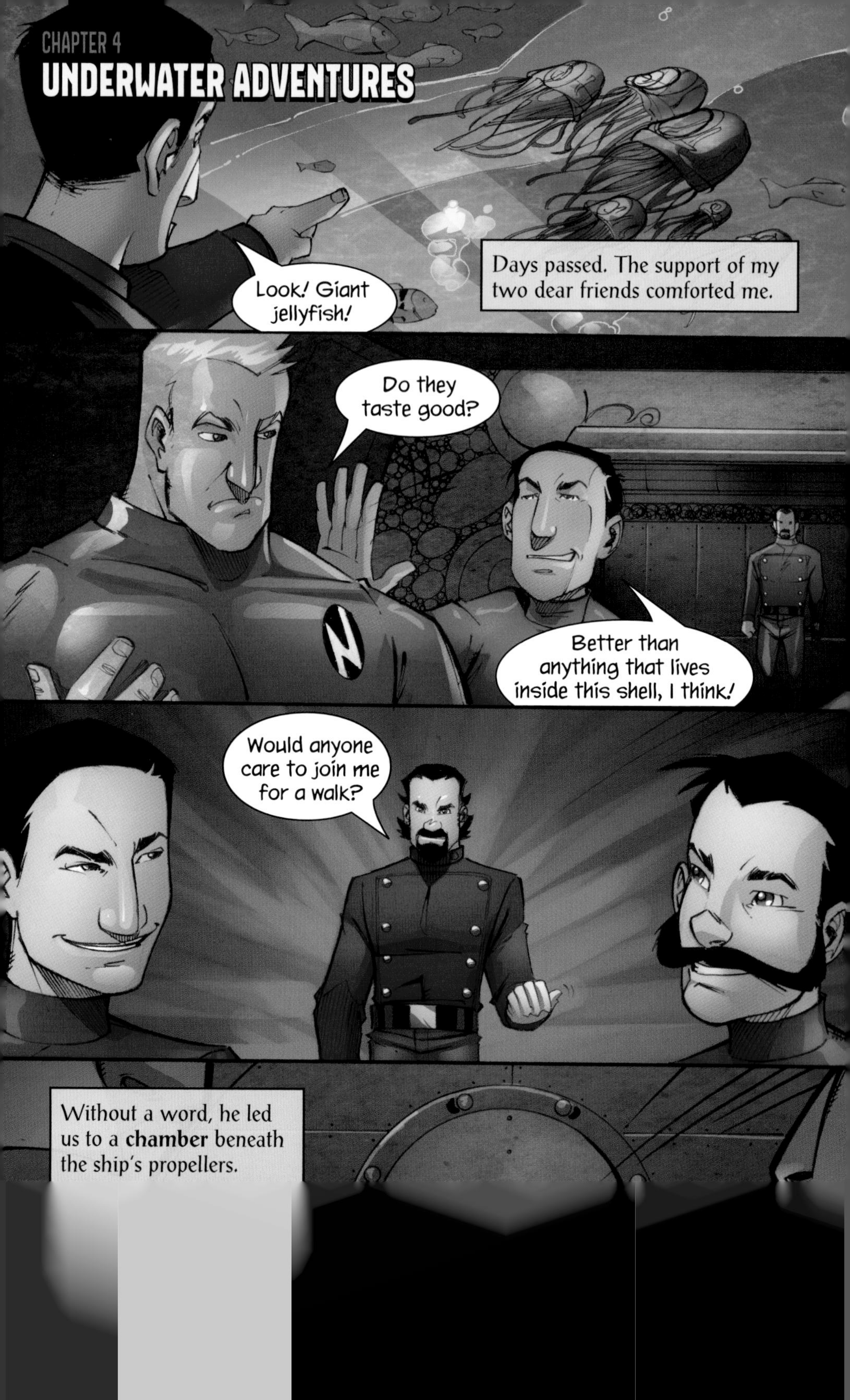
Days passed. The support of my two dear friends comforted me.
Look! Giant jellyfish!
Do they taste good?
Better than anything that lives inside this shell, I think!
Would anyone care to join me for a walk?
Without a word, he led us to a **chamber** beneath the ship's propellers.

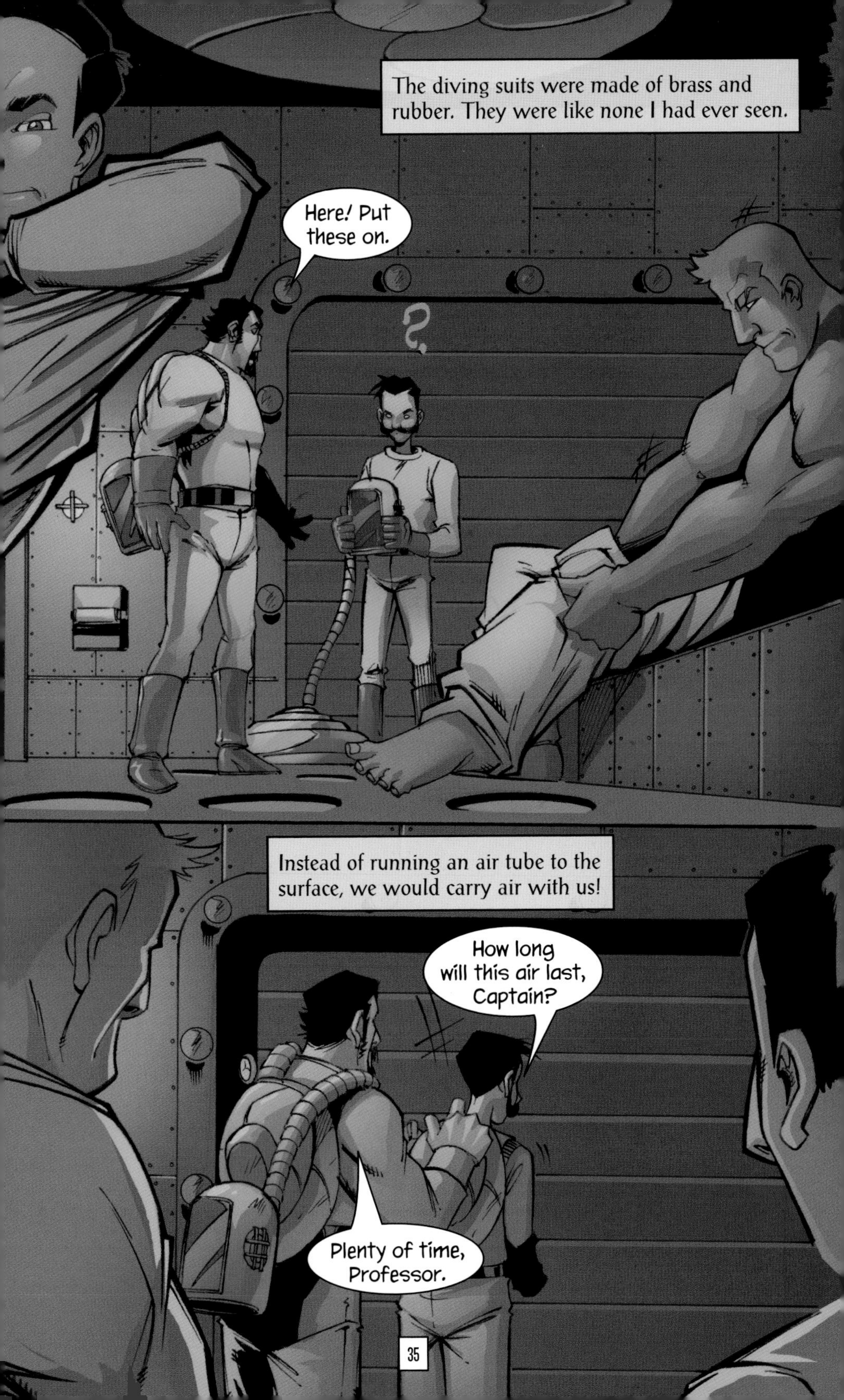
The diving suits were made of brass and rubber. They were like none I had ever seen.
Here! Put these on.
?
Instead of running an air tube to the surface, we would carry air with us!
How long will this air last, Captain?
Plenty of time, Professor.

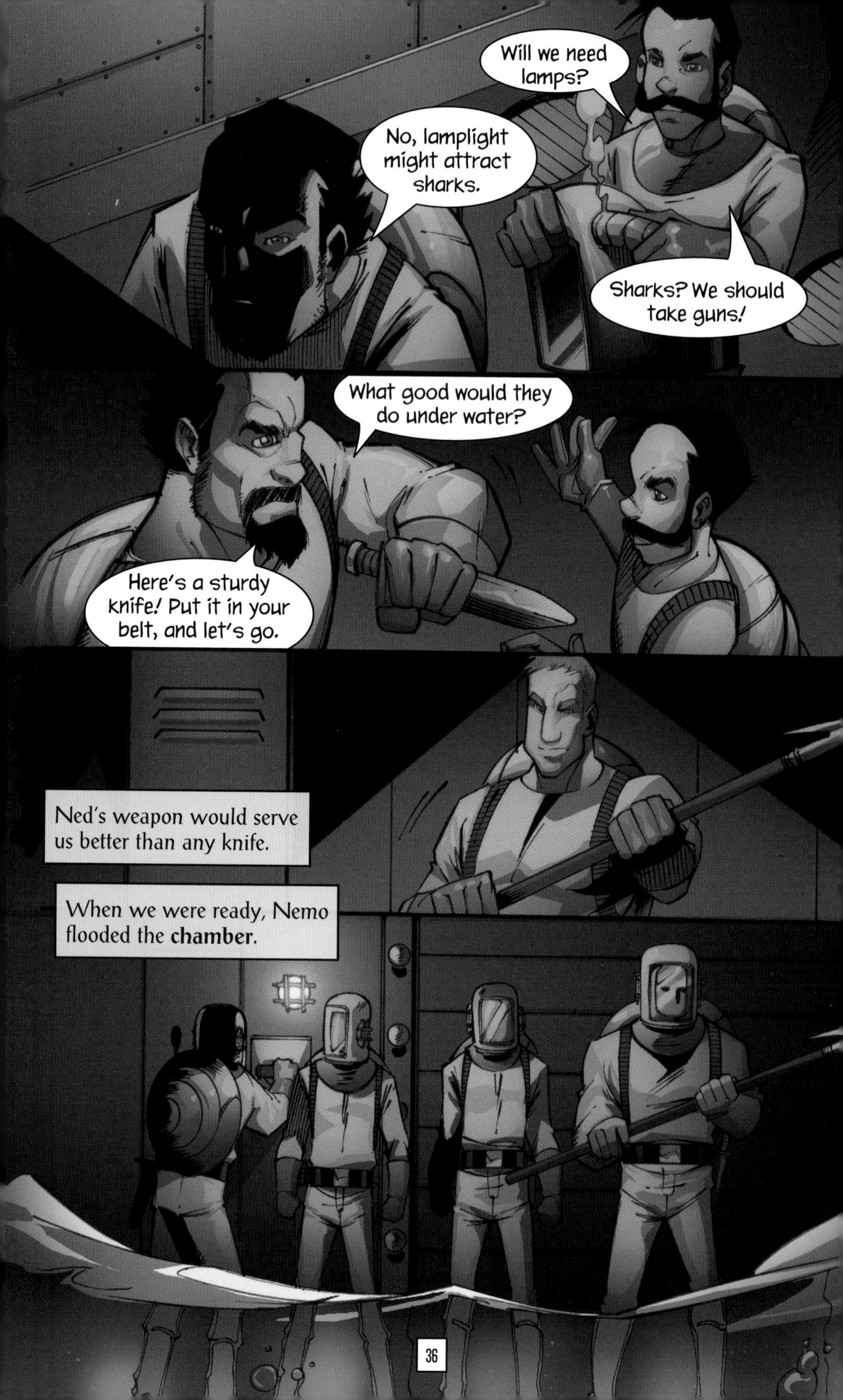

Will we need lamps?
No, lamplight might attract sharks.
Sharks? We should take guns!
What good would they do under water?
Here's a sturdy knife! Put it in your belt, and let's go.
Ned's weapon would serve us better than any knife.
When we were ready, Nemo flooded the **chamber**.

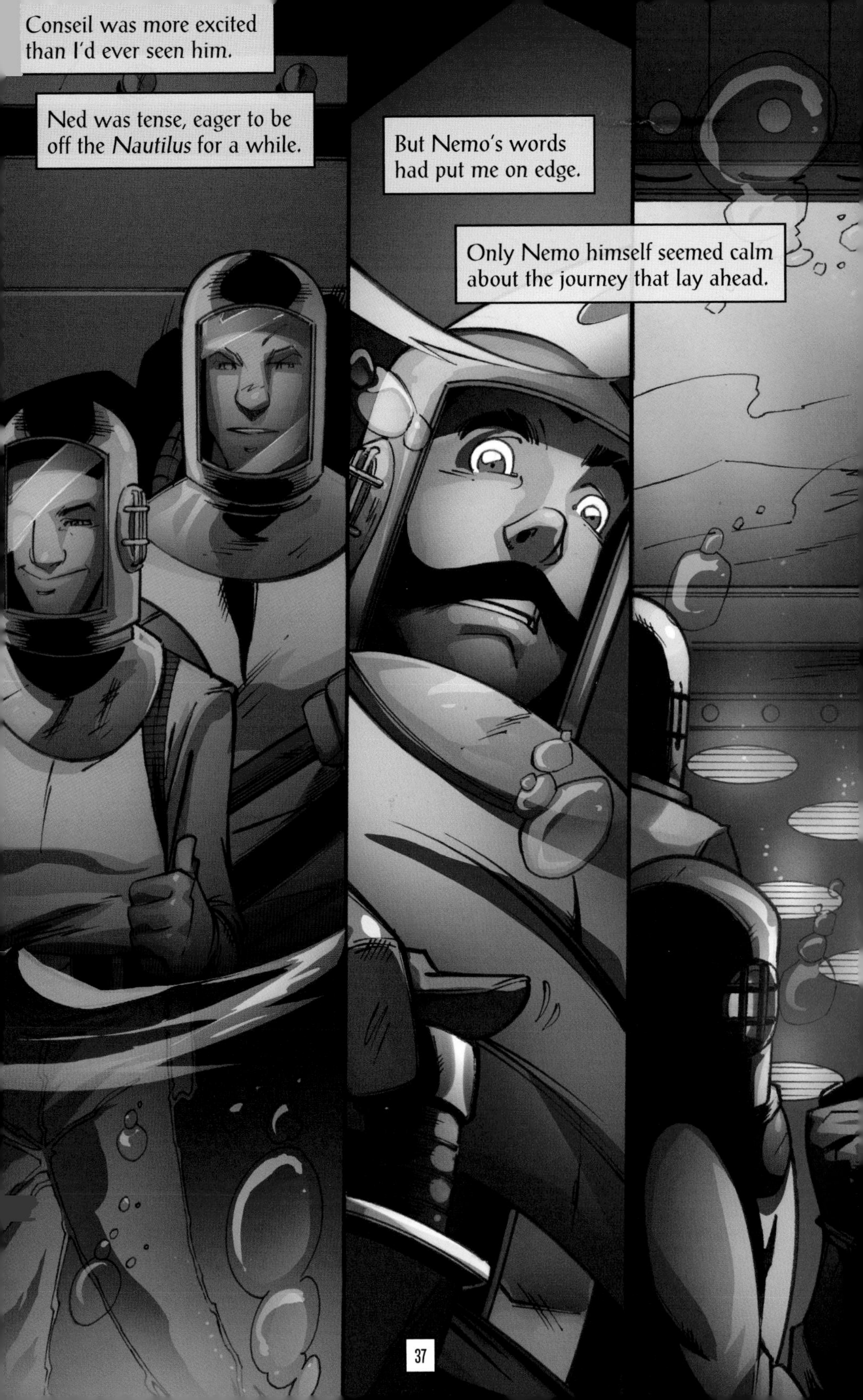
Conseil was more excited than I'd ever seen him.
Ned was tense, eager to be off the *Nautilus* for a while.
But Nemo's words had put me on edge.
Only Nemo himself seemed calm about the journey that lay ahead.

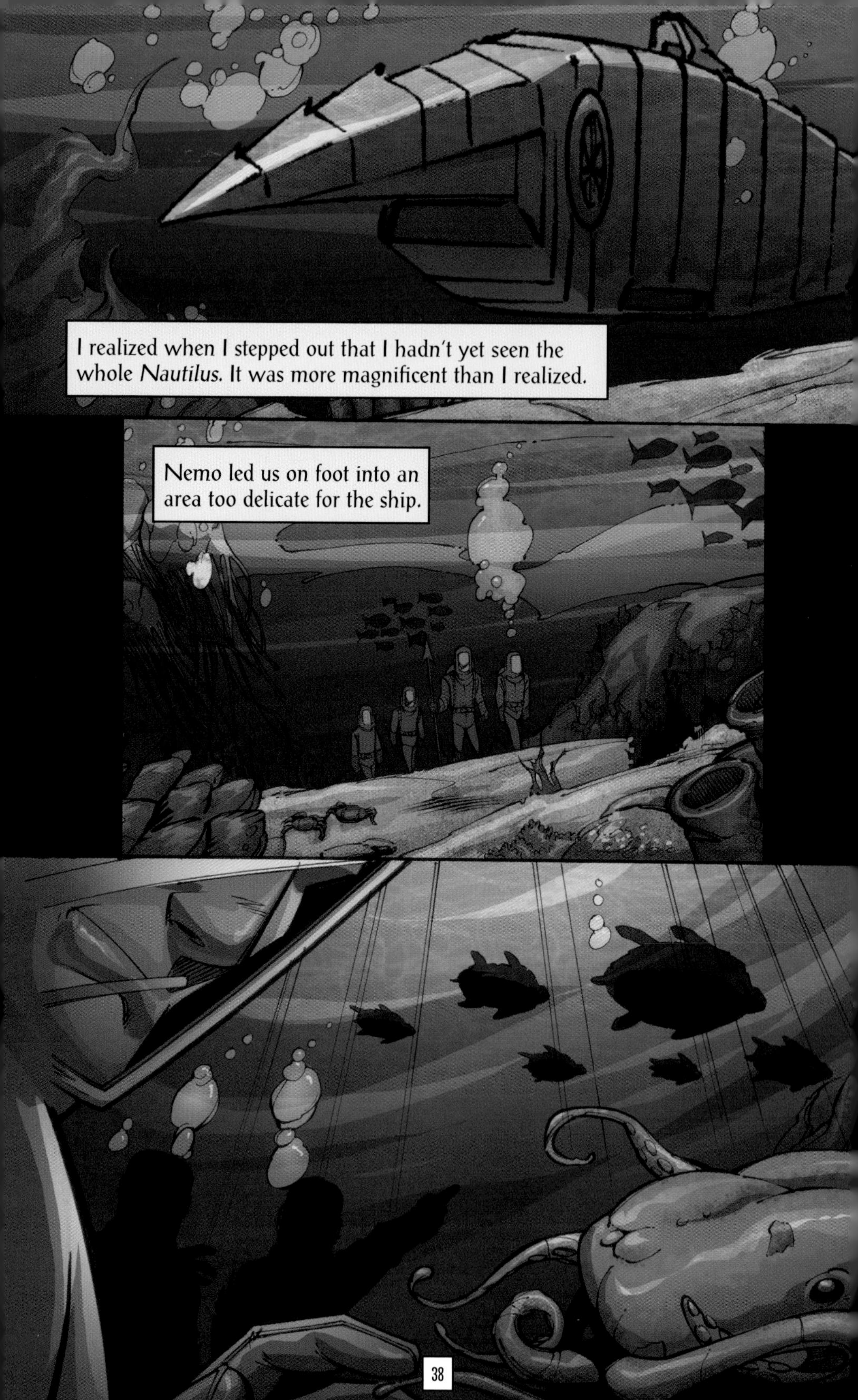
I realized when I stepped out that I hadn't yet seen the whole *Nautilus*. It was more magnificent than I realized.
Nemo led us on foot into an area too delicate for the ship.

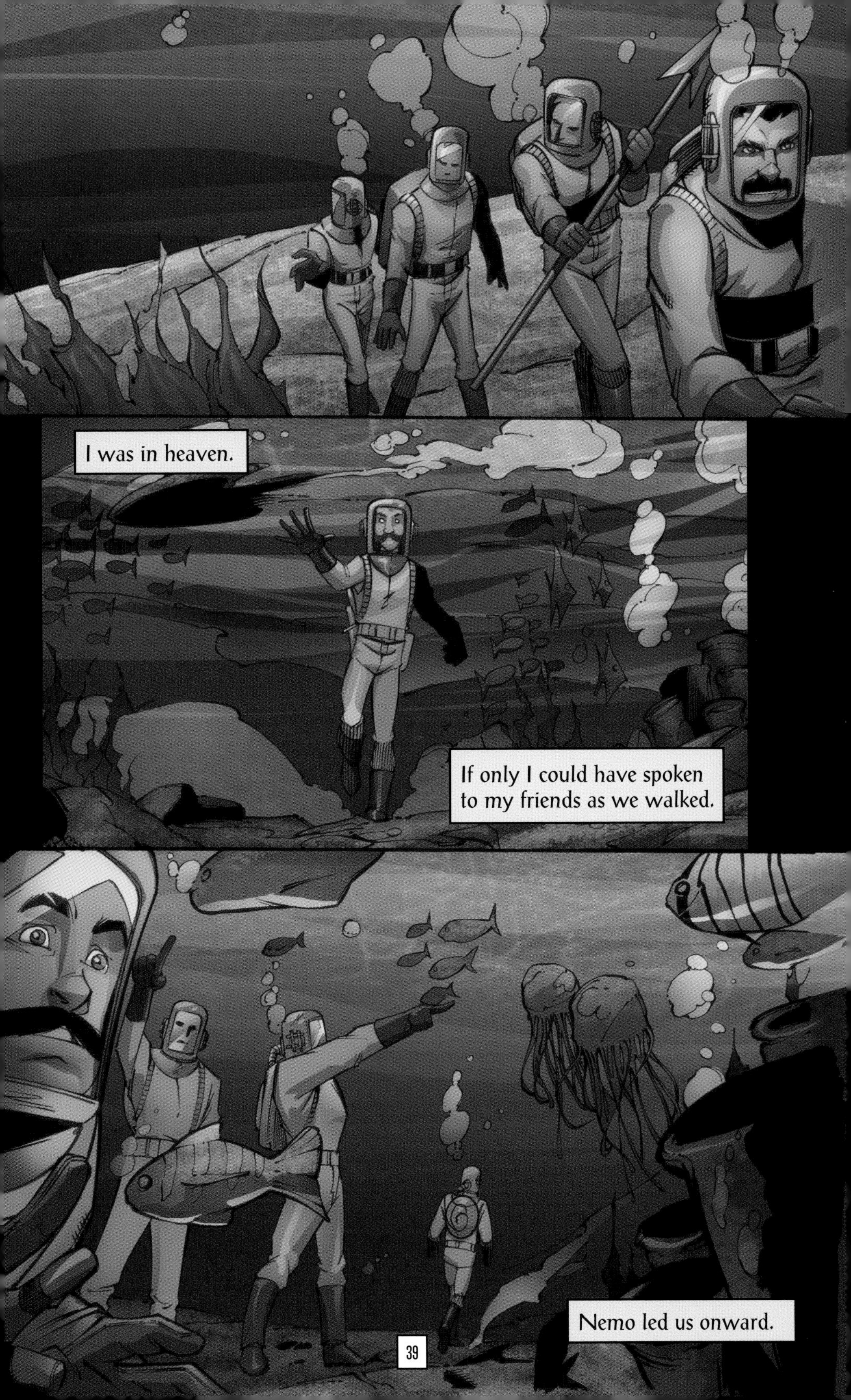
I was in heaven.
If only I could have spoken to my friends as we walked.
Nemo led us onward.

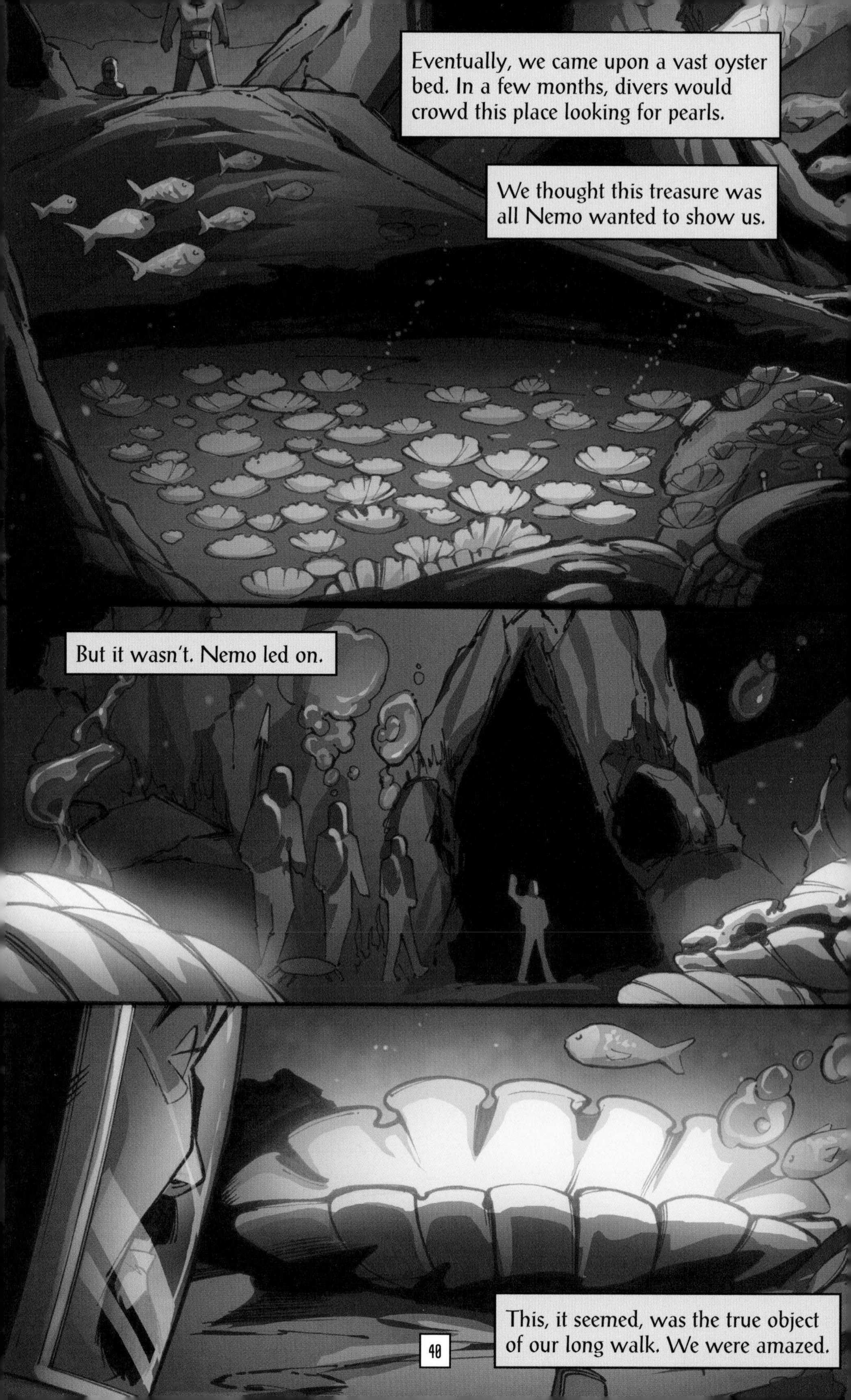
Eventually, we came upon a vast oyster bed. In a few months, divers would crowd this place looking for pearls.
We thought this treasure was all Nemo wanted to show us.
But it wasn't. Nemo led on.
This, it seemed, was the true object of our long walk. We were amazed.

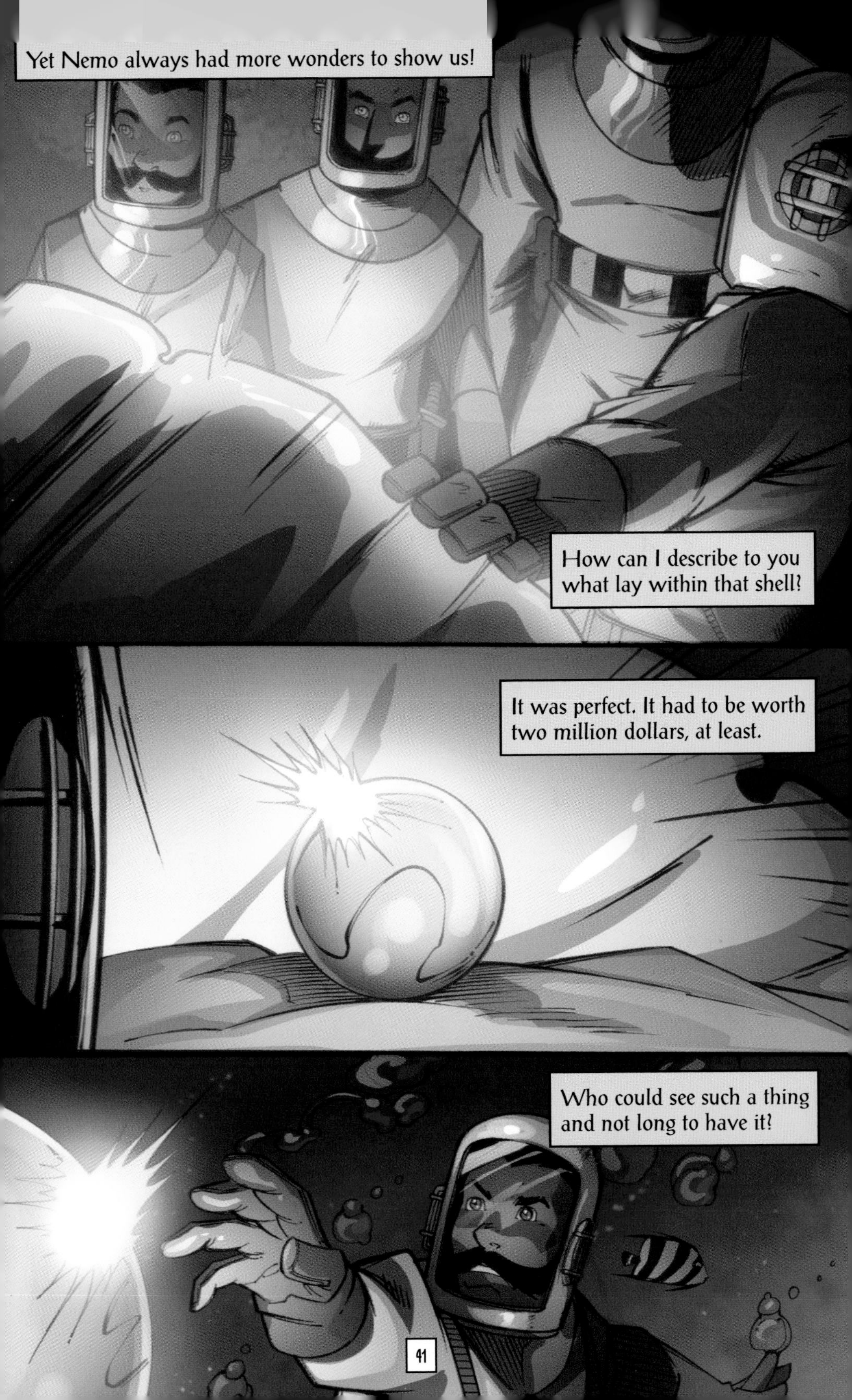
Yet Nemo always had more wonders to show us!
How can I describe to you what lay within that shell?
It was perfect. It had to be worth two million dollars, at least.
Who could see such a thing and not long to have it?

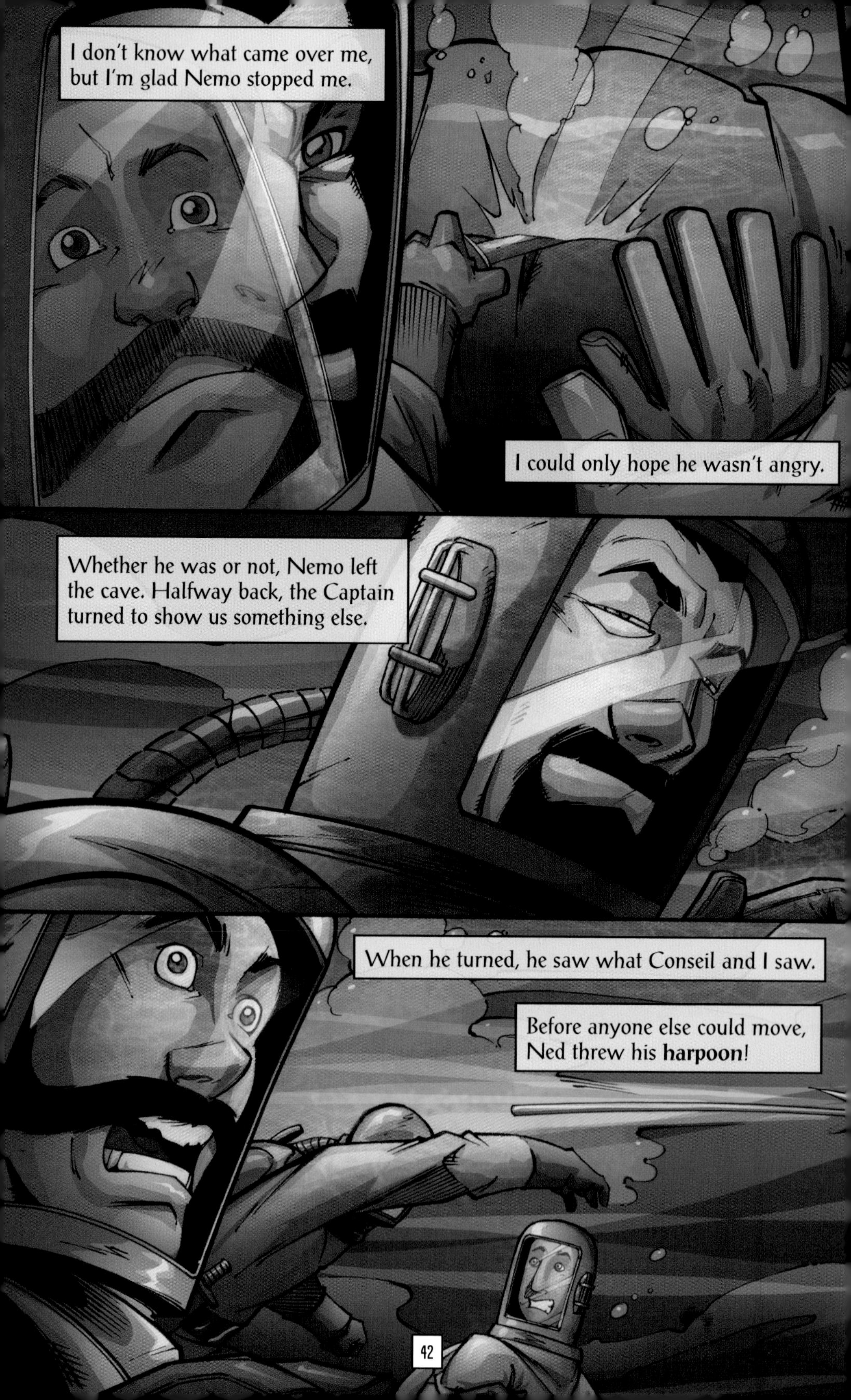
I don't know what came over me, but I'm glad Nemo stopped me.
I could only hope he wasn't angry.
Whether he was or not, Nemo left the cave. Halfway back, the Captain turned to show us something else.
When he turned, he saw what Conseil and I saw.
Before anyone else could move, Ned threw his **harpoon**!

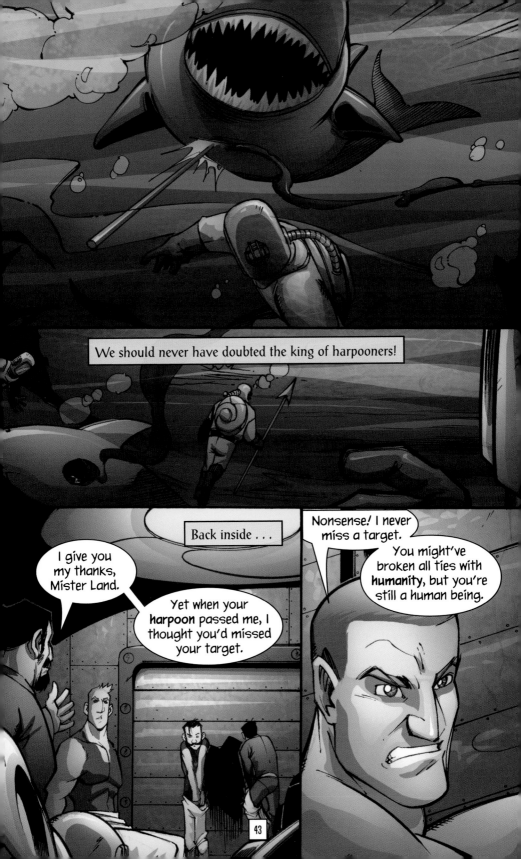

We should never have doubted the king of harpooners!

Back inside . . .

I give you my thanks, Mister Land.

Yet when your **harpoon** passed me, I thought you'd missed your target.

Nonsense! I never miss a target.

You might've broken all ties with **humanity**, but you're still a human being.

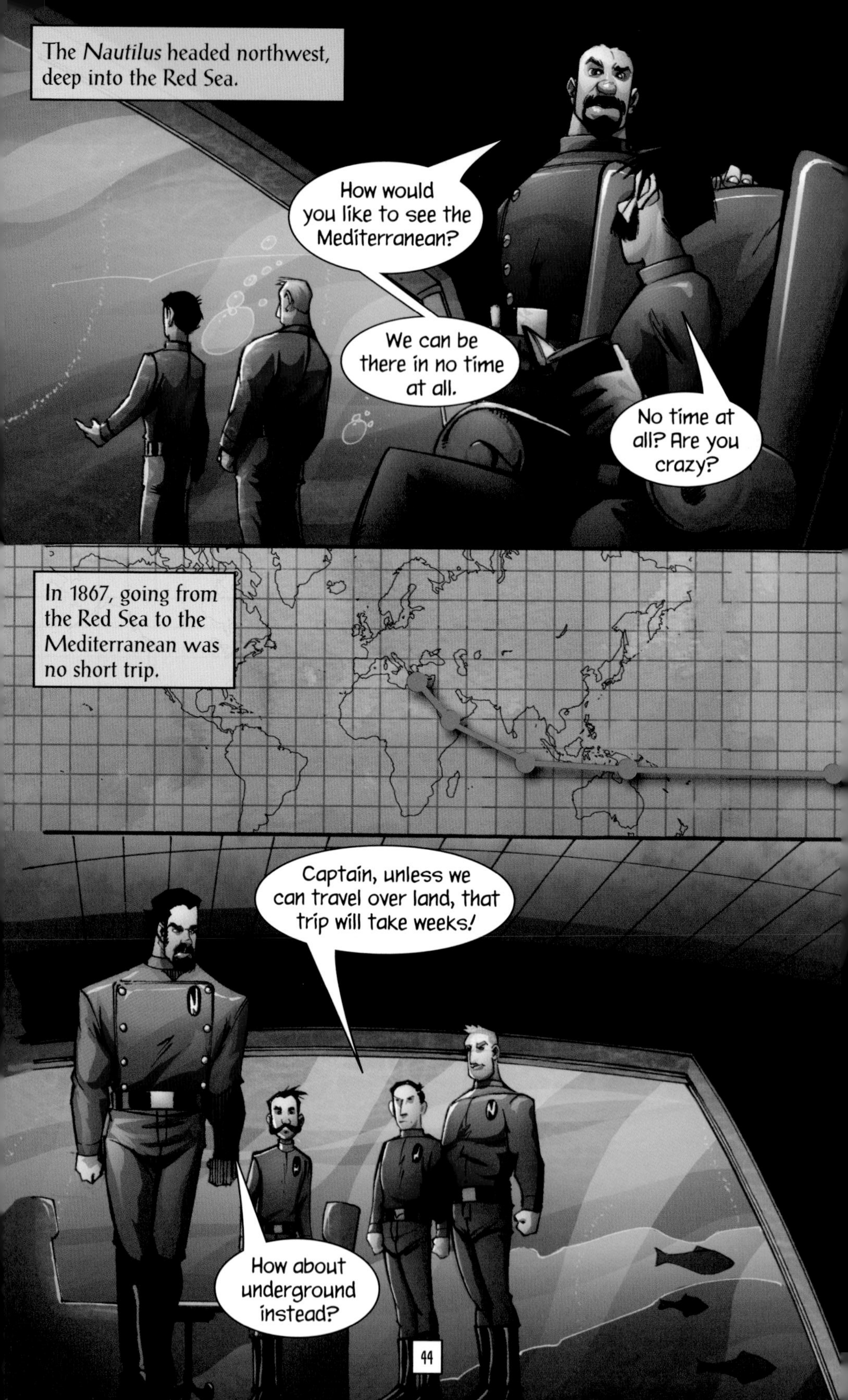
The *Nautilus* headed northwest, deep into the Red Sea.
How would you like to see the Mediterranean?
We can be there in no time at all.
No time at all? Are you crazy?
In 1867, going from the Red Sea to the Mediterranean was no short trip.
Captain, unless we can travel over land, that trip will take weeks!
How about underground instead?

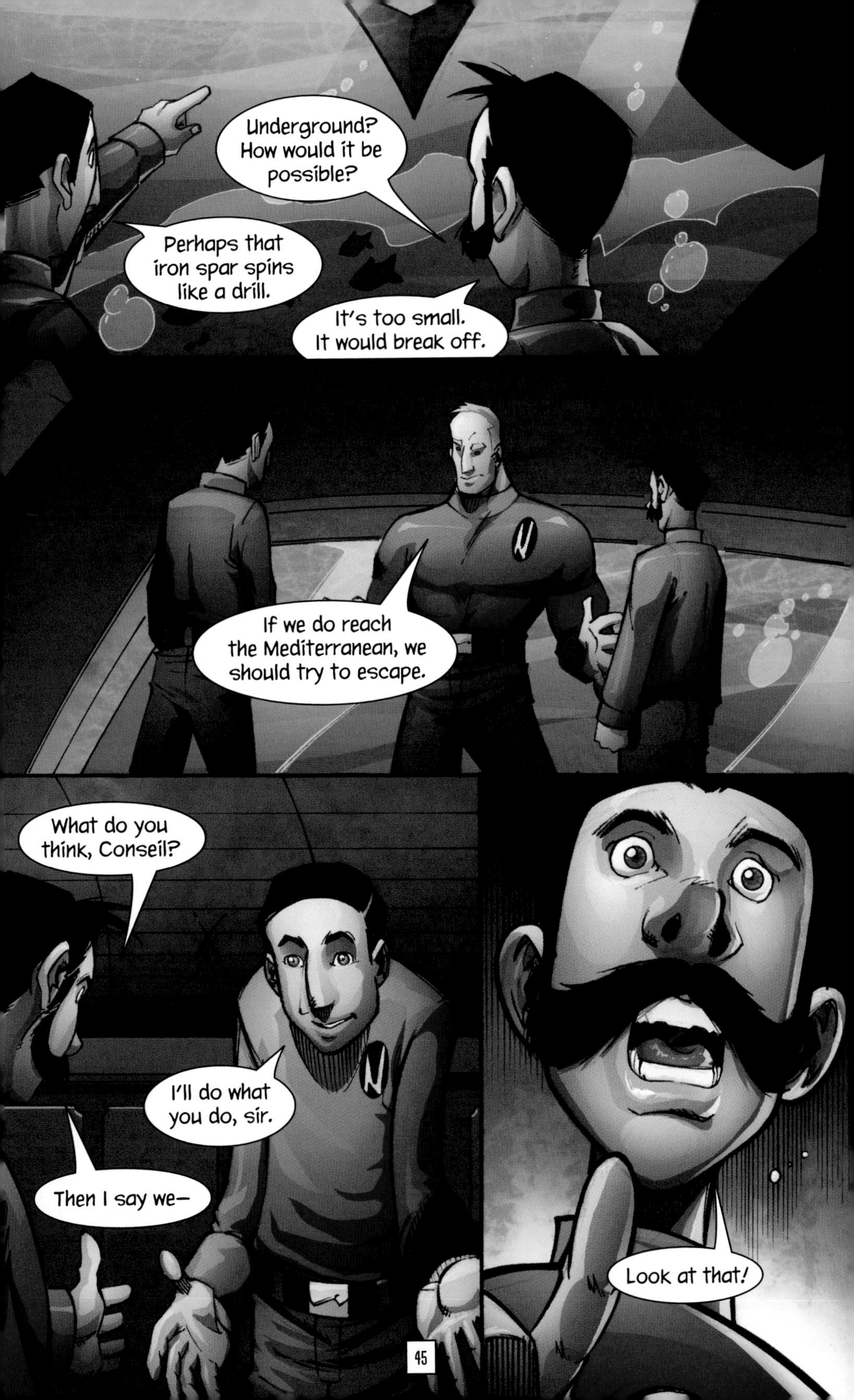
Underground? How would it be possible?
Perhaps that iron spar spins like a drill.
It's too small. It would break off.
If we do reach the Mediterranean, we should try to escape.
What do you think, Conseil?
I'll do what you do, sir.
Then I say we—
Look at that!

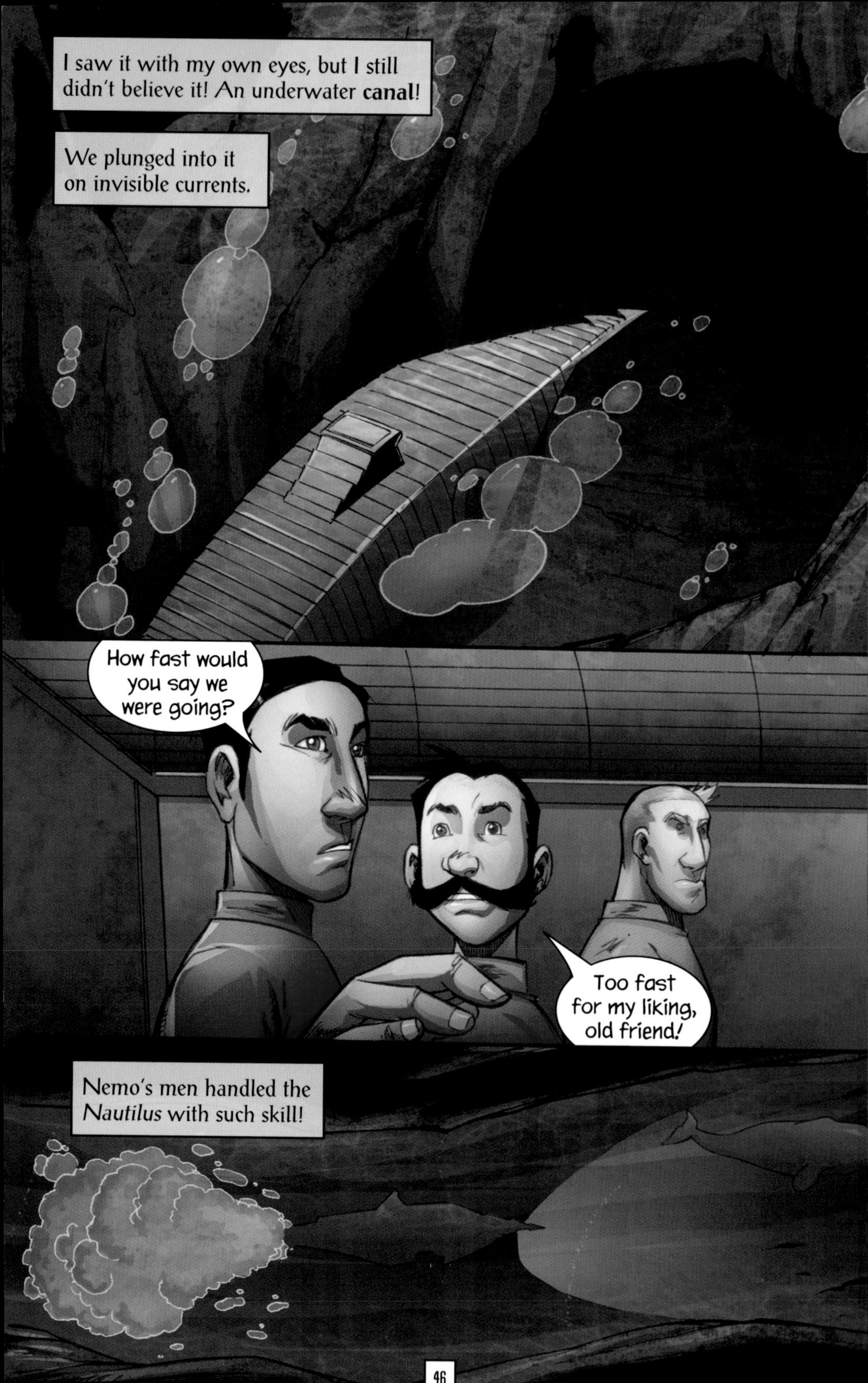
I saw it with my own eyes, but I still didn't believe it! An underwater **canal**!
We plunged into it on invisible currents.
How fast would you say we were going?
Too fast for my liking, old friend!
Nemo's men handled the *Nautilus* with such skill!

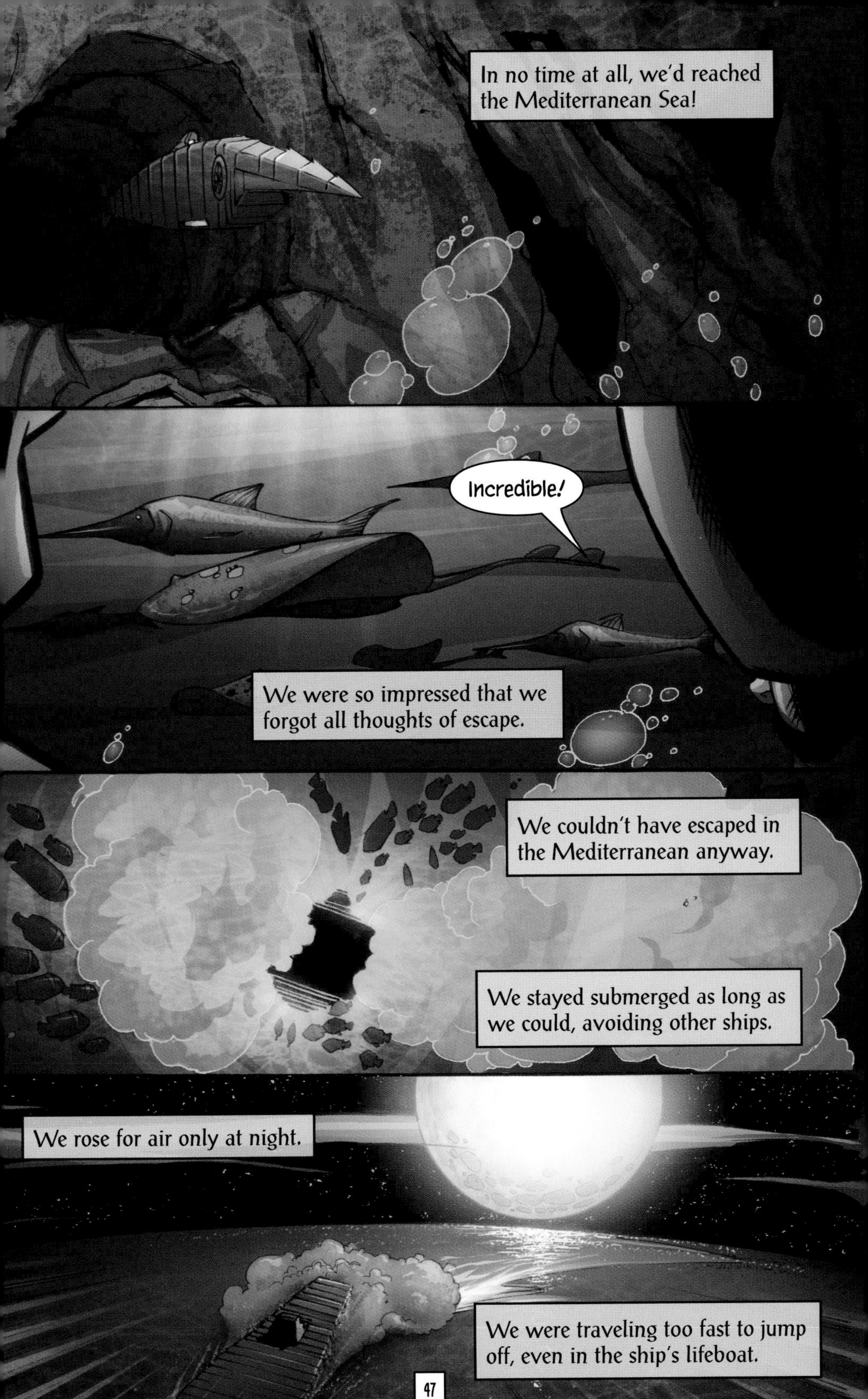
In no time at all, we'd reached the Mediterranean Sea!
Incredible!
We were so impressed that we forgot all thoughts of escape.
We couldn't have escaped in the Mediterranean anyway.
We stayed submerged as long as we could, avoiding other ships.
We rose for air only at night.
We were traveling too fast to jump off, even in the ship's lifeboat.

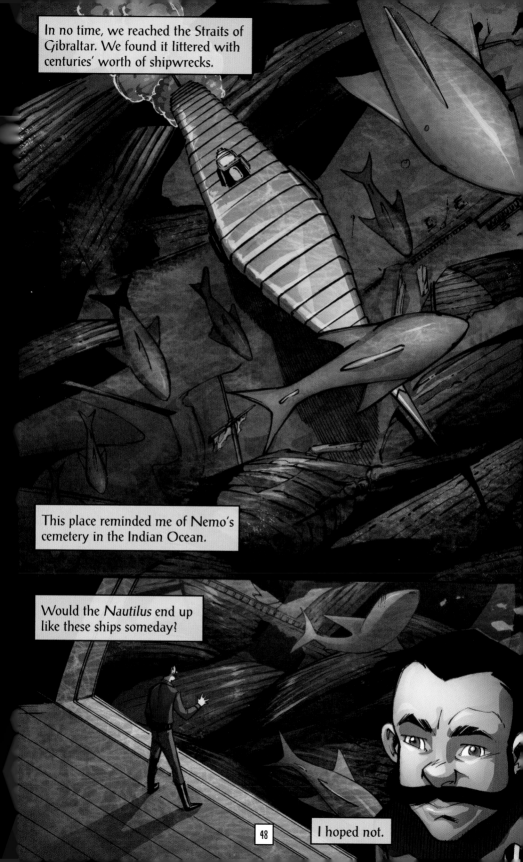

In no time, we reached the Straits of Gibraltar. We found it littered with centuries' worth of shipwrecks.

This place reminded me of Nemo's cemetery in the Indian Ocean.

Would the *Nautilus* end up like these ships someday!

I hoped not.

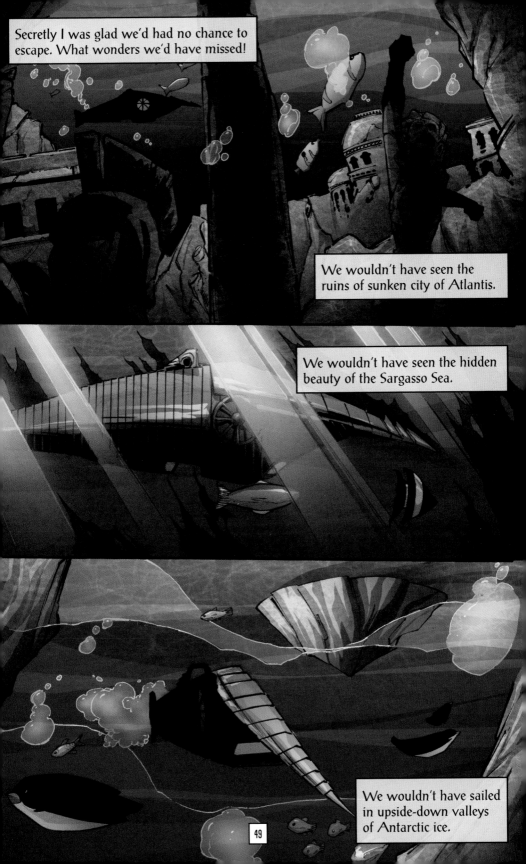

Secretly I was glad we'd had no chance to escape. What wonders we'd have missed!

We wouldn't have seen the ruins of sunken city of Atlantis.

We wouldn't have seen the hidden beauty of the Sargasso Sea.

We wouldn't have sailed in upside-down valleys of Antarctic ice.

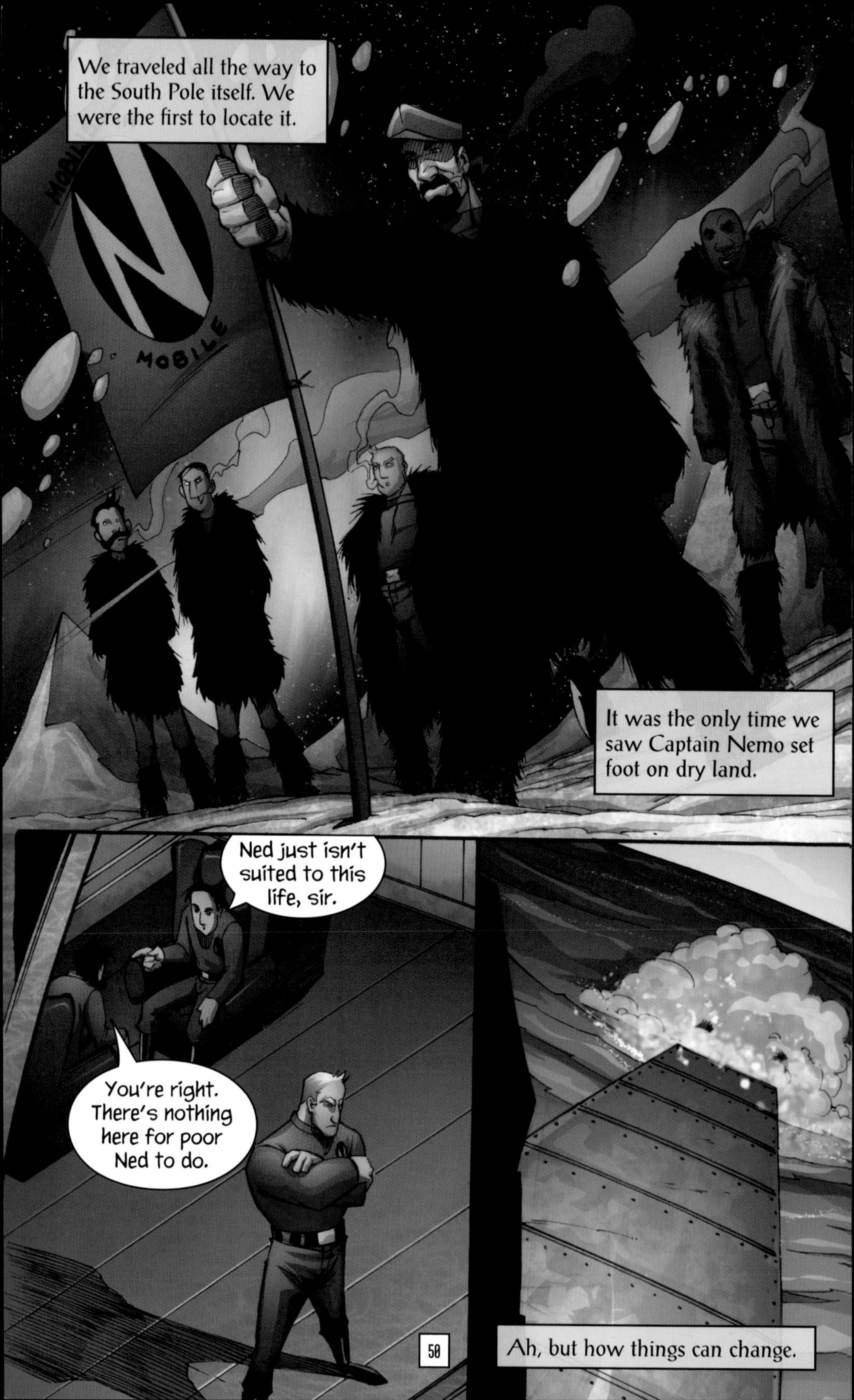
We traveled all the way to the South Pole itself. We were the first to locate it.
MOBILE
MOBILE
It was the only time we saw Captain Nemo set foot on dry land.
Ned just isn't suited to this life, sir.
You're right. There's nothing here for poor Ned to do.
Ah, but how things can change.

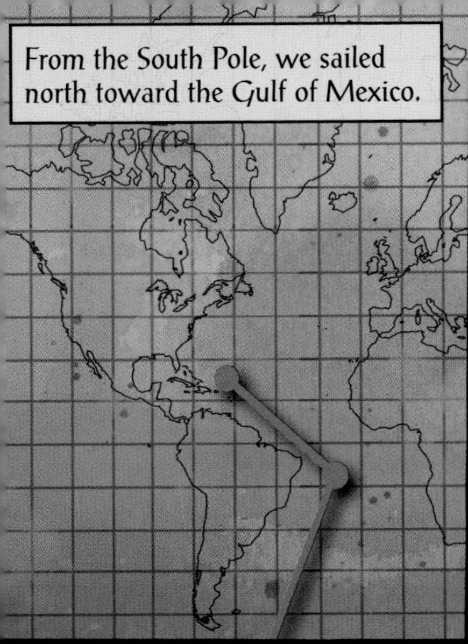
From the South Pole, we sailed north toward the Gulf of Mexico.

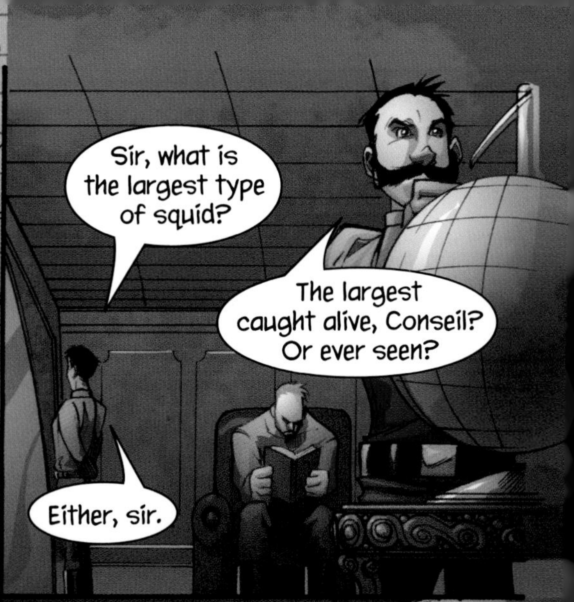
Sir, what is the largest type of squid?
The largest caught alive, Conseil? Or ever seen?
Either, sir.

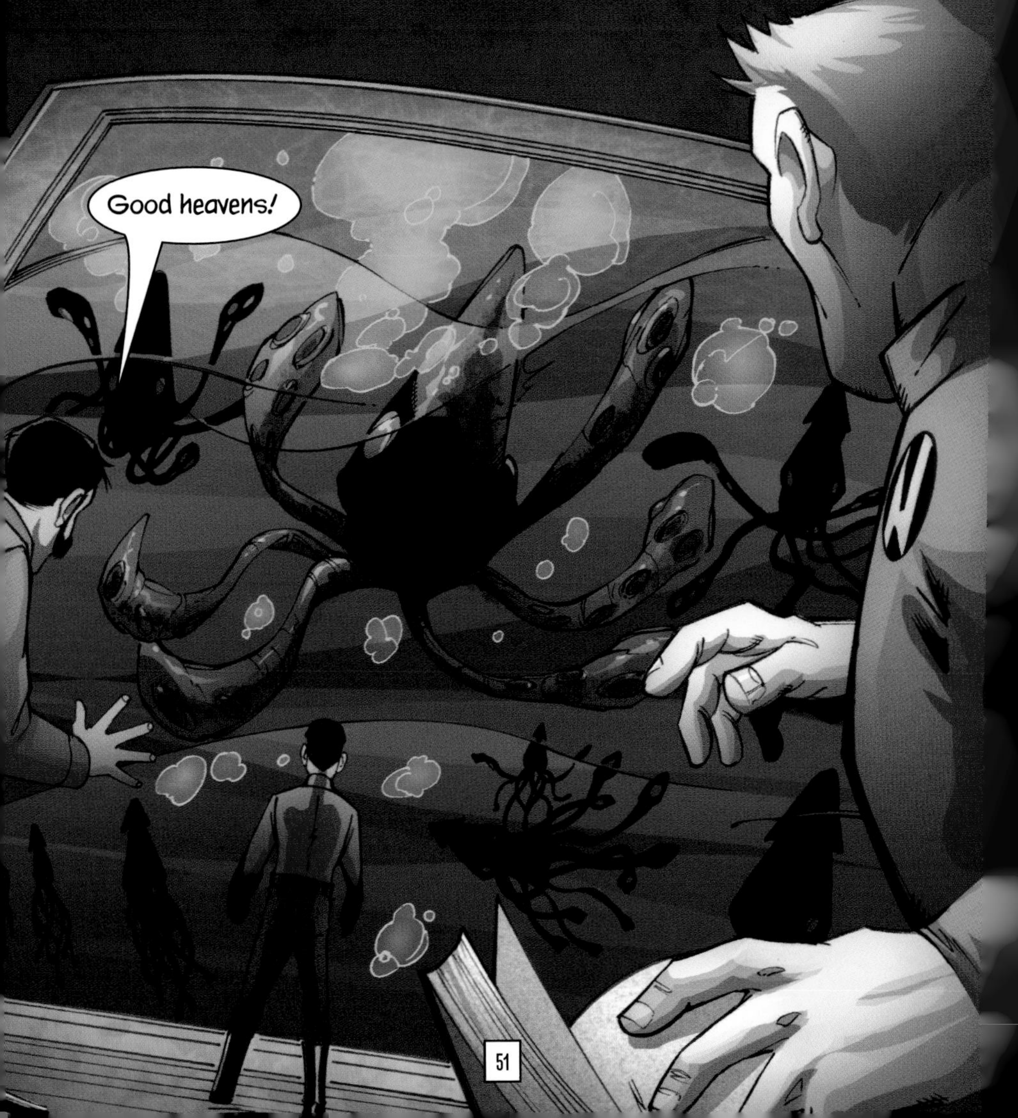
Good heavens!

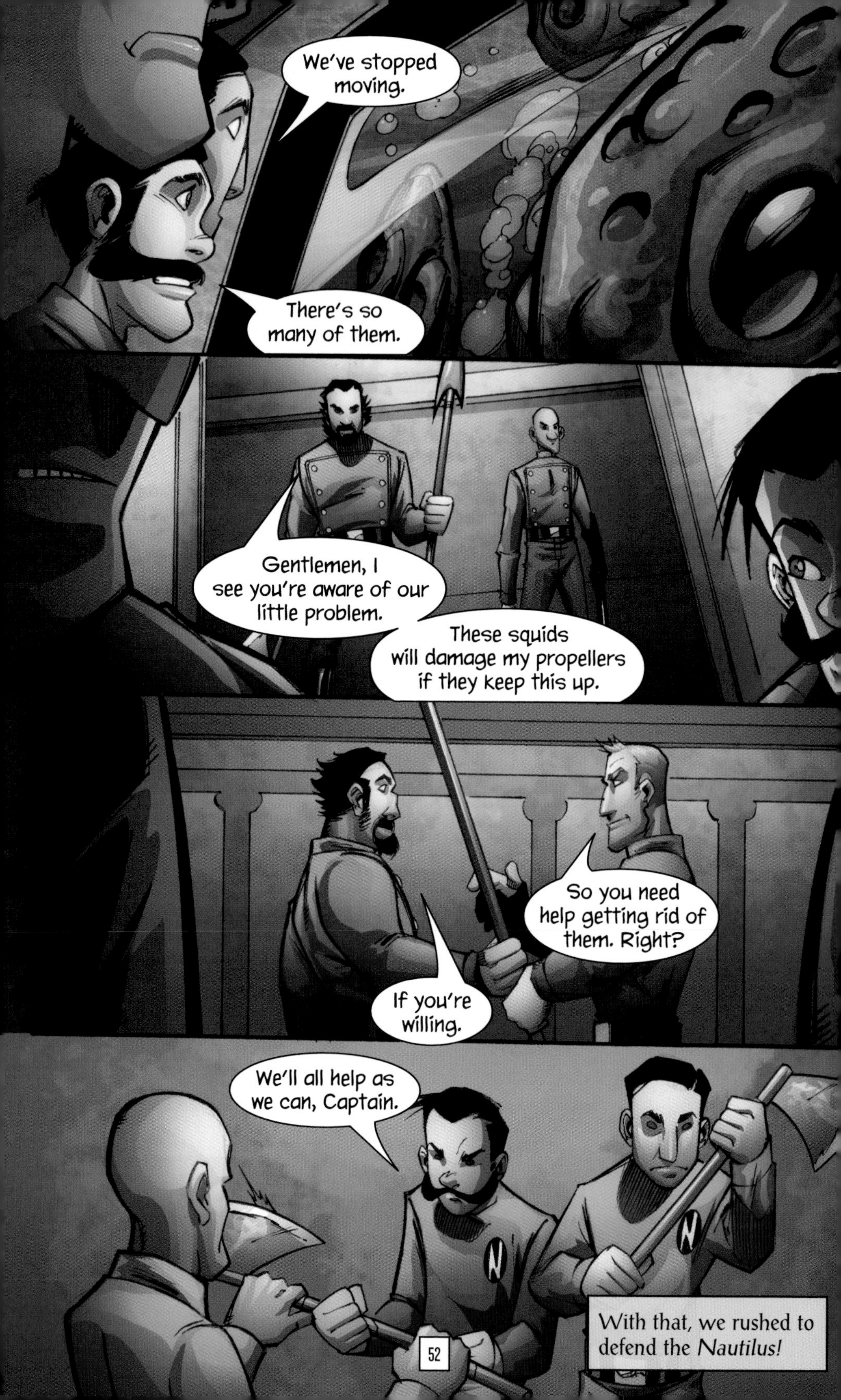
We've stopped moving.
There's so many of them.
Gentlemen, I see you're aware of our little problem.
These squids will damage my propellers if they keep this up.
So you need help getting rid of them. Right?
If you're willing.
We'll all help as we can, Captain.
With that, we rushed to defend the *Nautilus!*

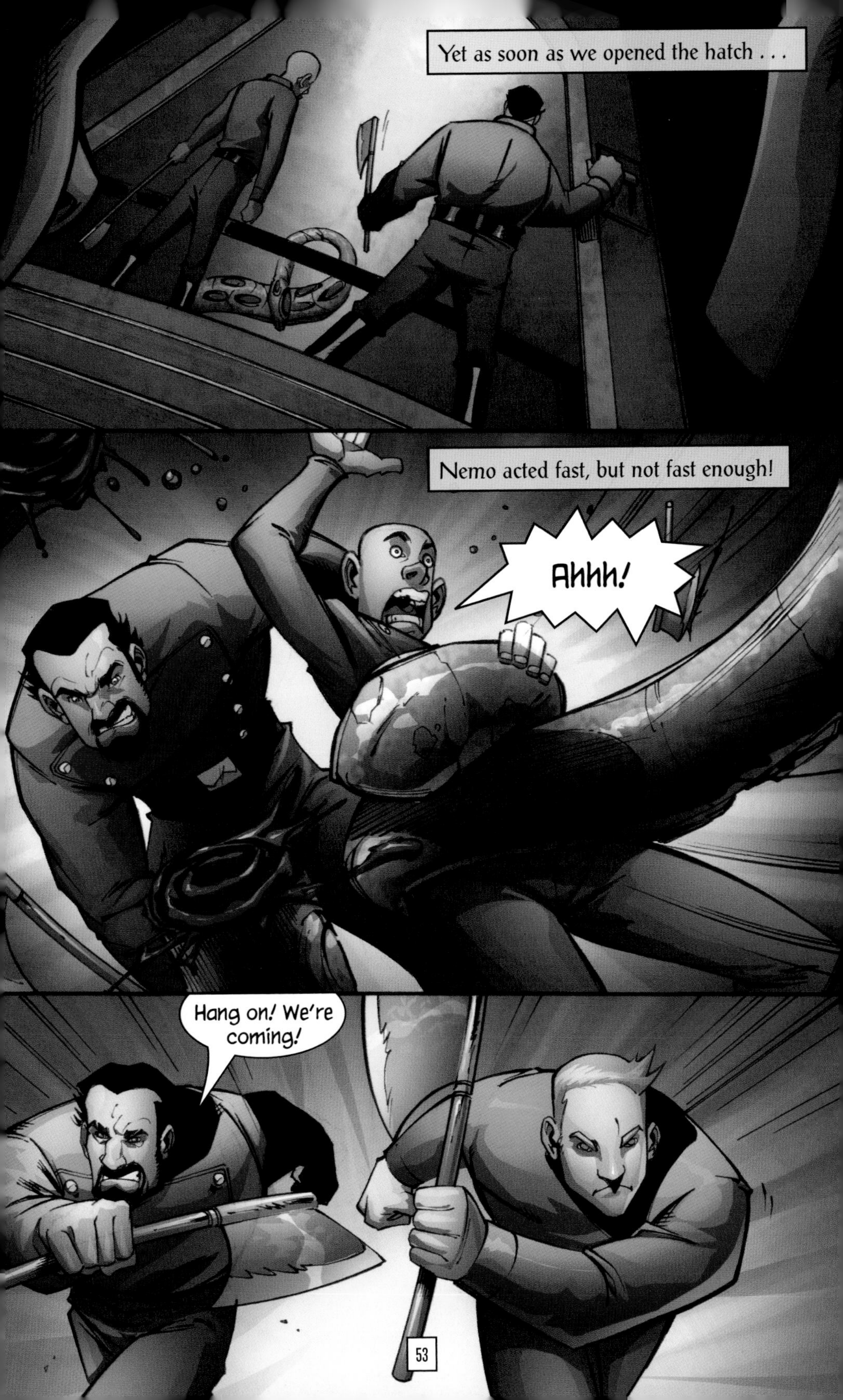
Yet as soon as we opened the hatch . . .
Nemo acted fast, but not fast enough!
Ahhh!
Hang on! We're coming!

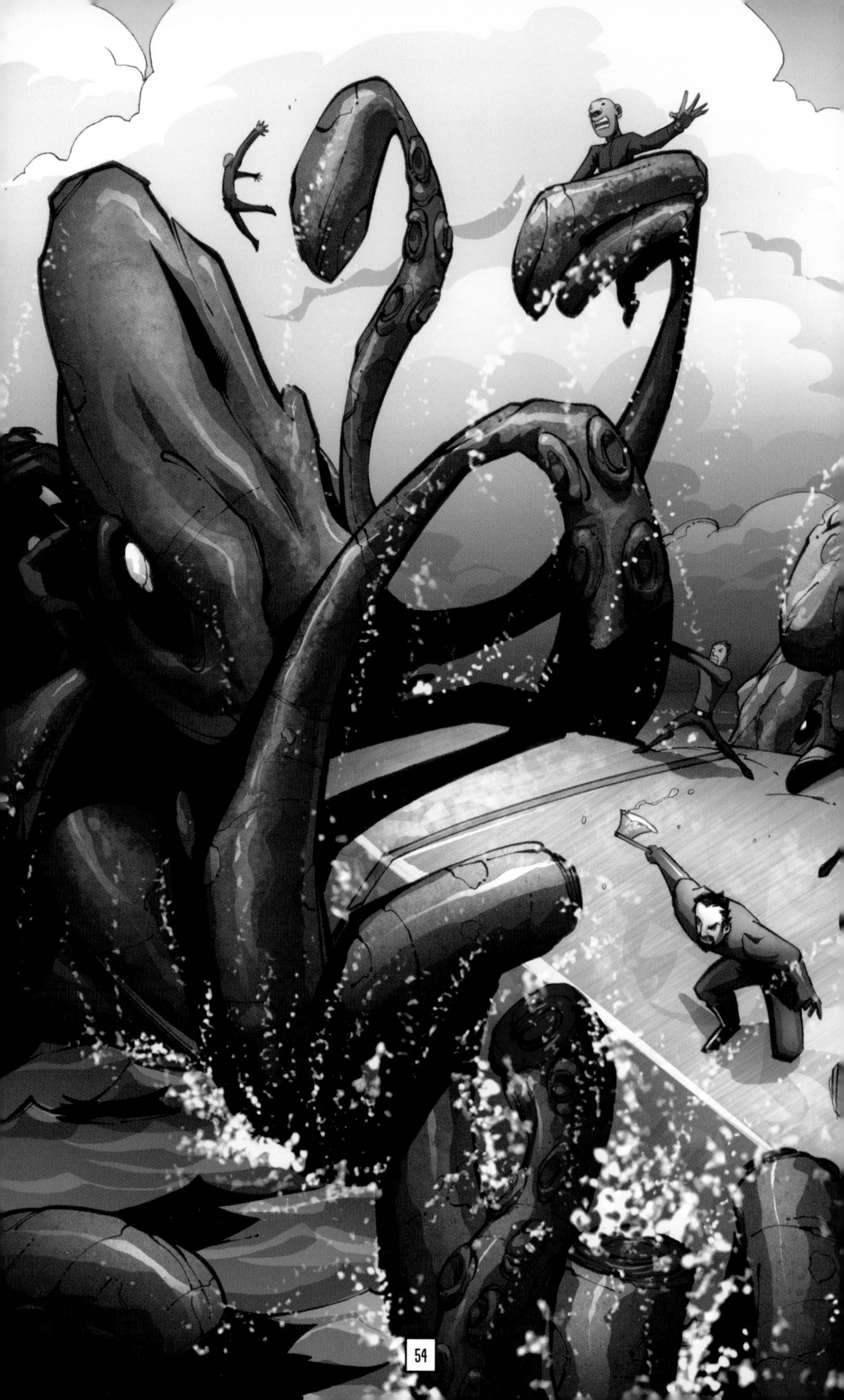

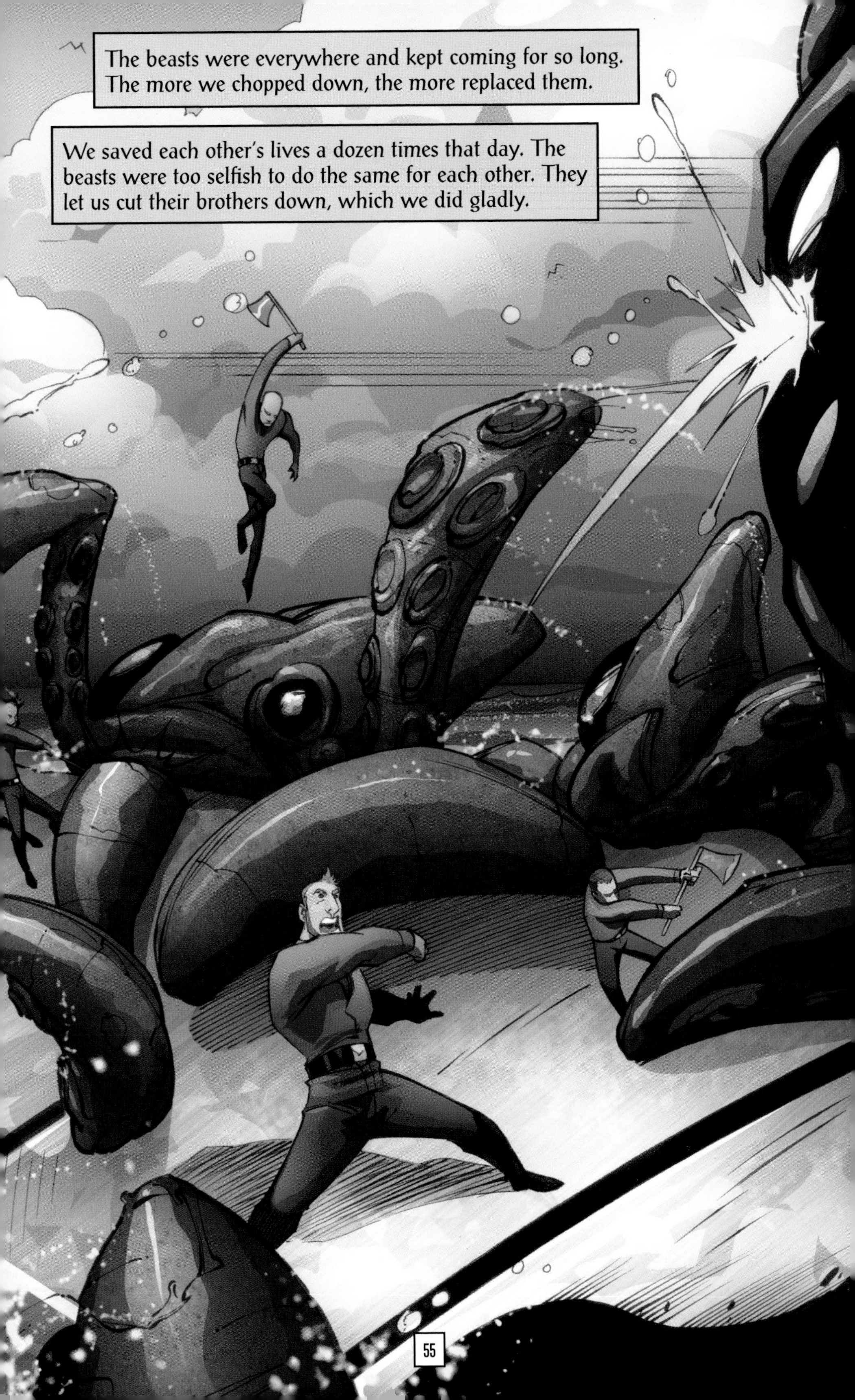
The beasts were everywhere and kept coming for so long. The more we chopped down, the more replaced them.
We saved each other's lives a dozen times that day. The beasts were too selfish to do the same for each other. They let us cut their brothers down, which we did gladly.

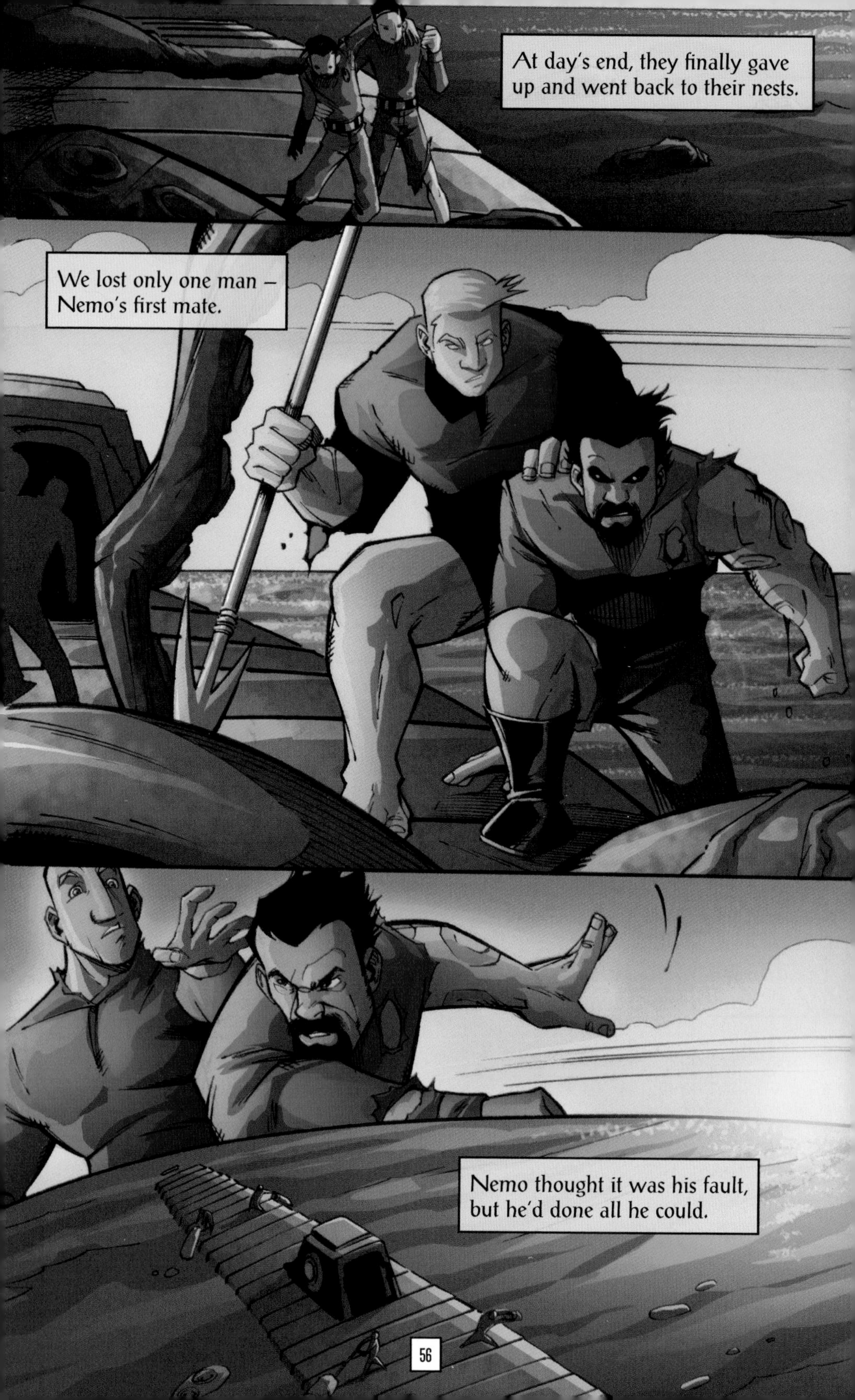
At day's end, they finally gave up and went back to their nests.
We lost only one man – Nemo's first mate.
Nemo thought it was his fault, but he'd done all he could.

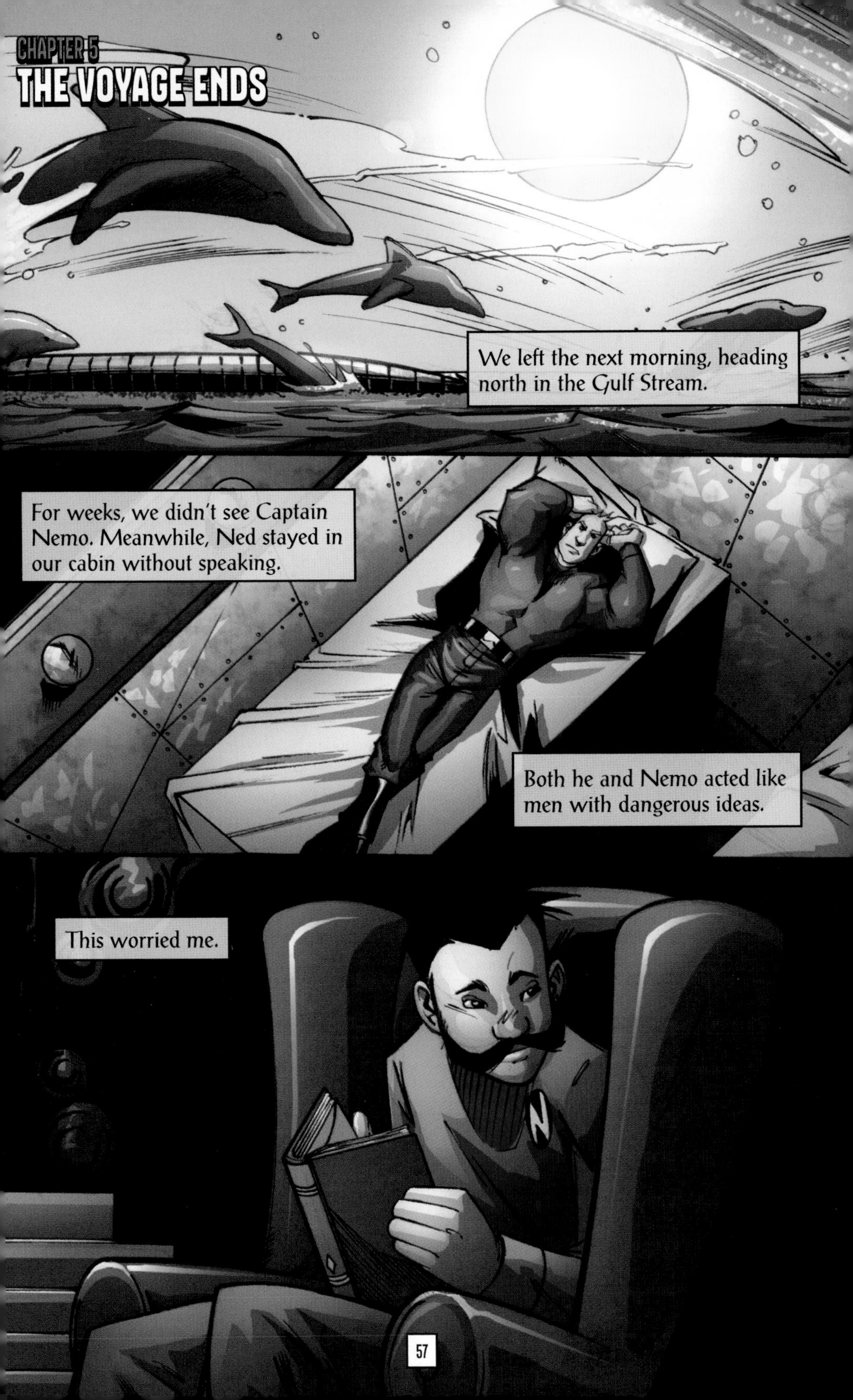
CHAPTER 5
THE VOYAGE ENDS
We left the next morning, heading north in the Gulf Stream.
For weeks, we didn't see Captain Nemo. Meanwhile, Ned stayed in our cabin without speaking.
Both he and Nemo acted like men with dangerous ideas.
This worried me.

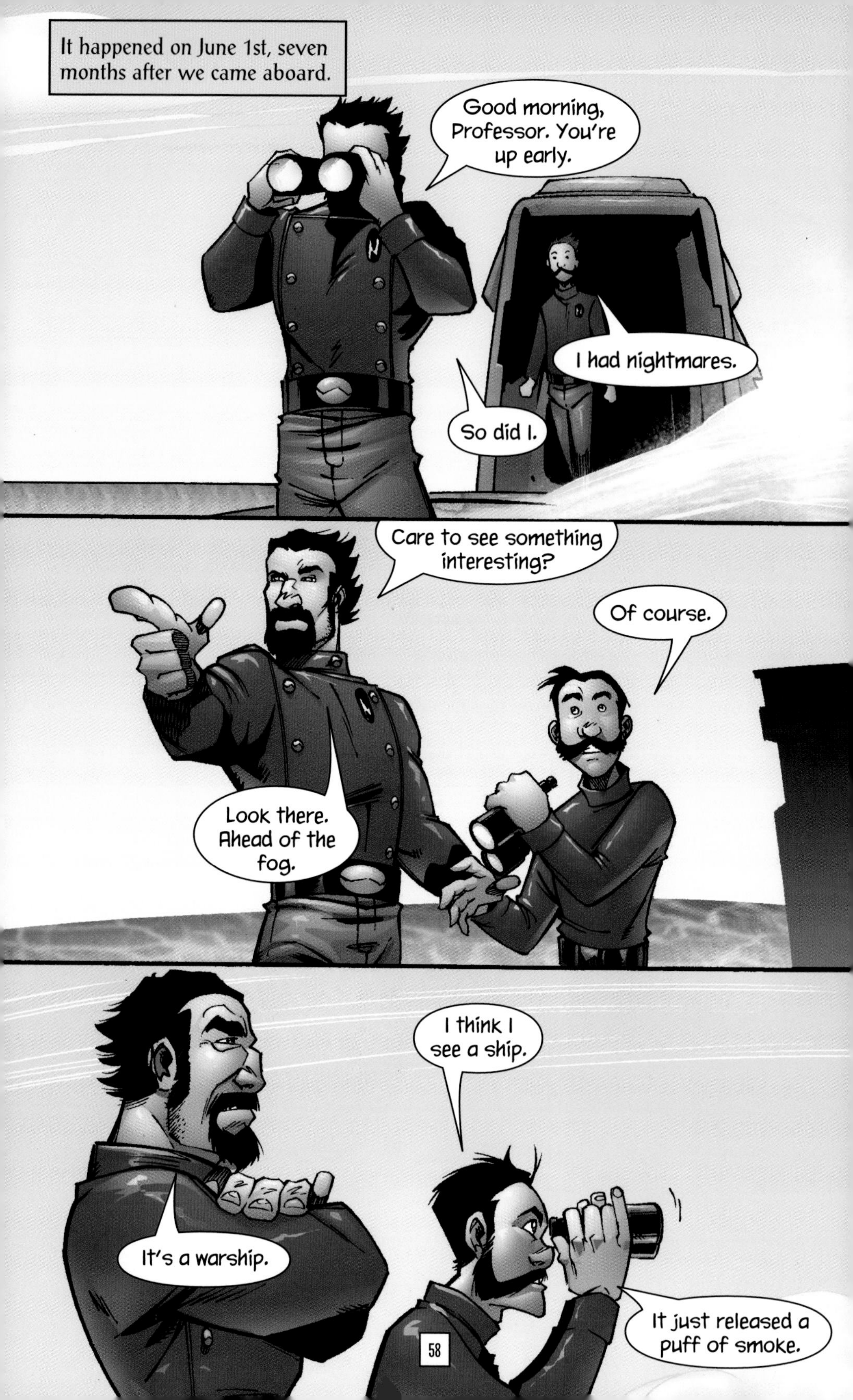
It happened on June 1st, seven months after we came aboard.
Good morning, Professor. You're up early.
I had nightmares.
So did I.
Care to see something interesting?
Of course.
Look there. Ahead of the fog.
I think I see a ship.
It's a warship.
It just released a puff of smoke.

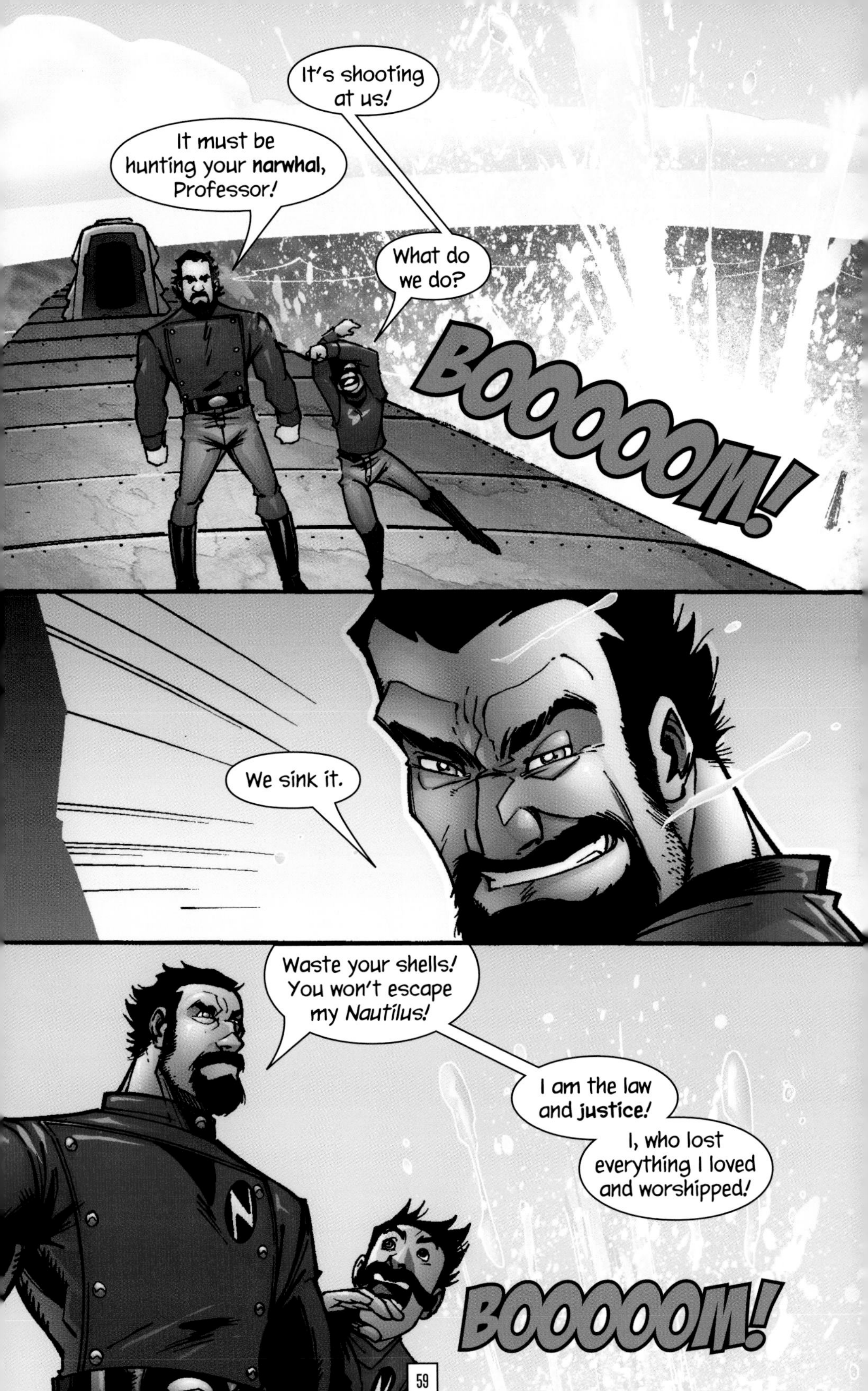
It's shooting at us!
It must be hunting your **narwhal**, Professor!
What do we do?
BOOOOOM!
We sink it.
Waste your shells! You won't escape my *Nautilus*!
I am the law and **justice**!
I, who lost everything I loved and worshipped!
BOOOOOM!

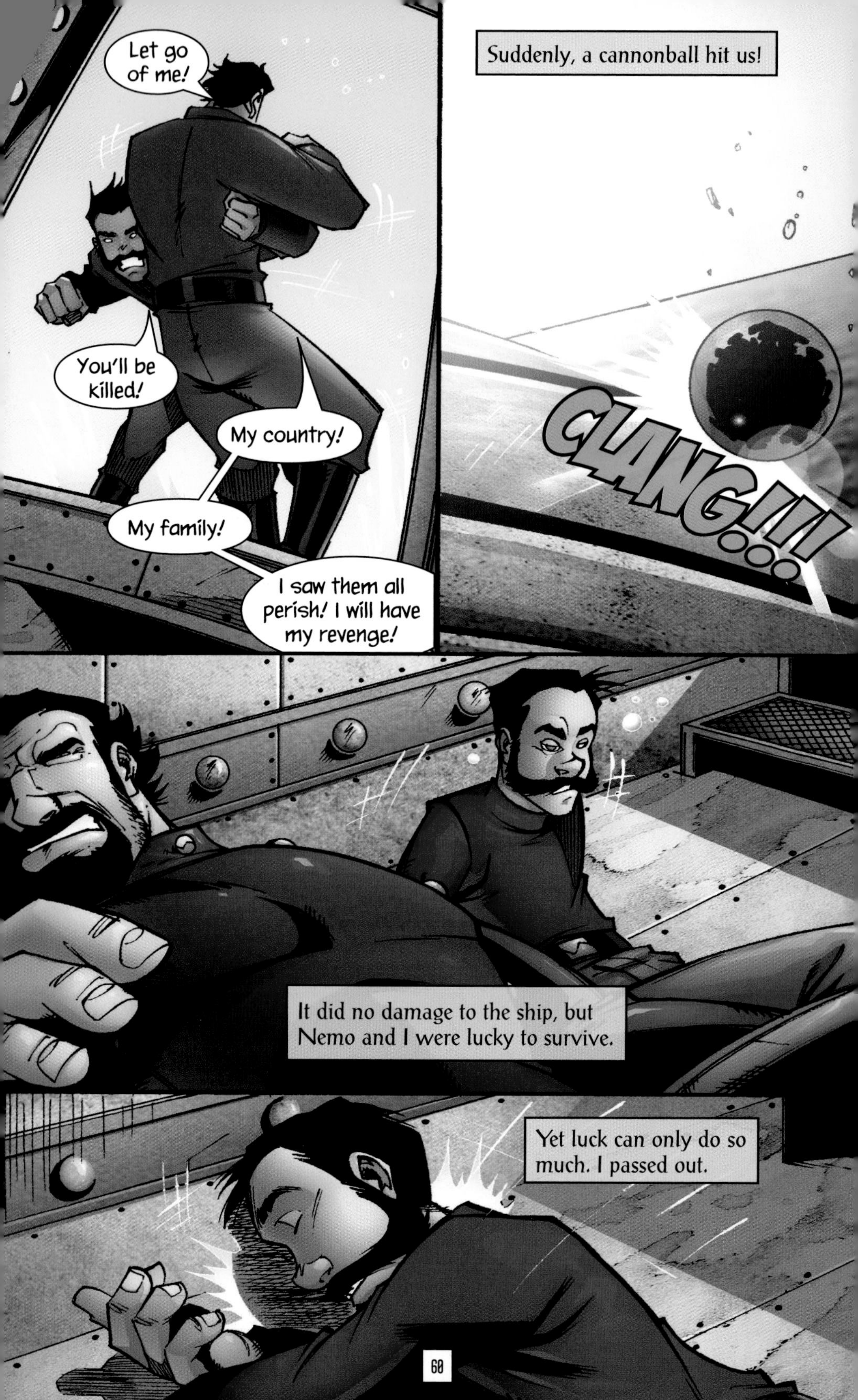

Let go of me!
You'll be killed!
My country!
My family!
I saw them all perish! I will have my revenge!
Suddenly, a cannonball hit us!
CLANG!!!...
It did no damage to the ship, but Nemo and I were lucky to survive.
Yet luck can only do so much. I passed out.

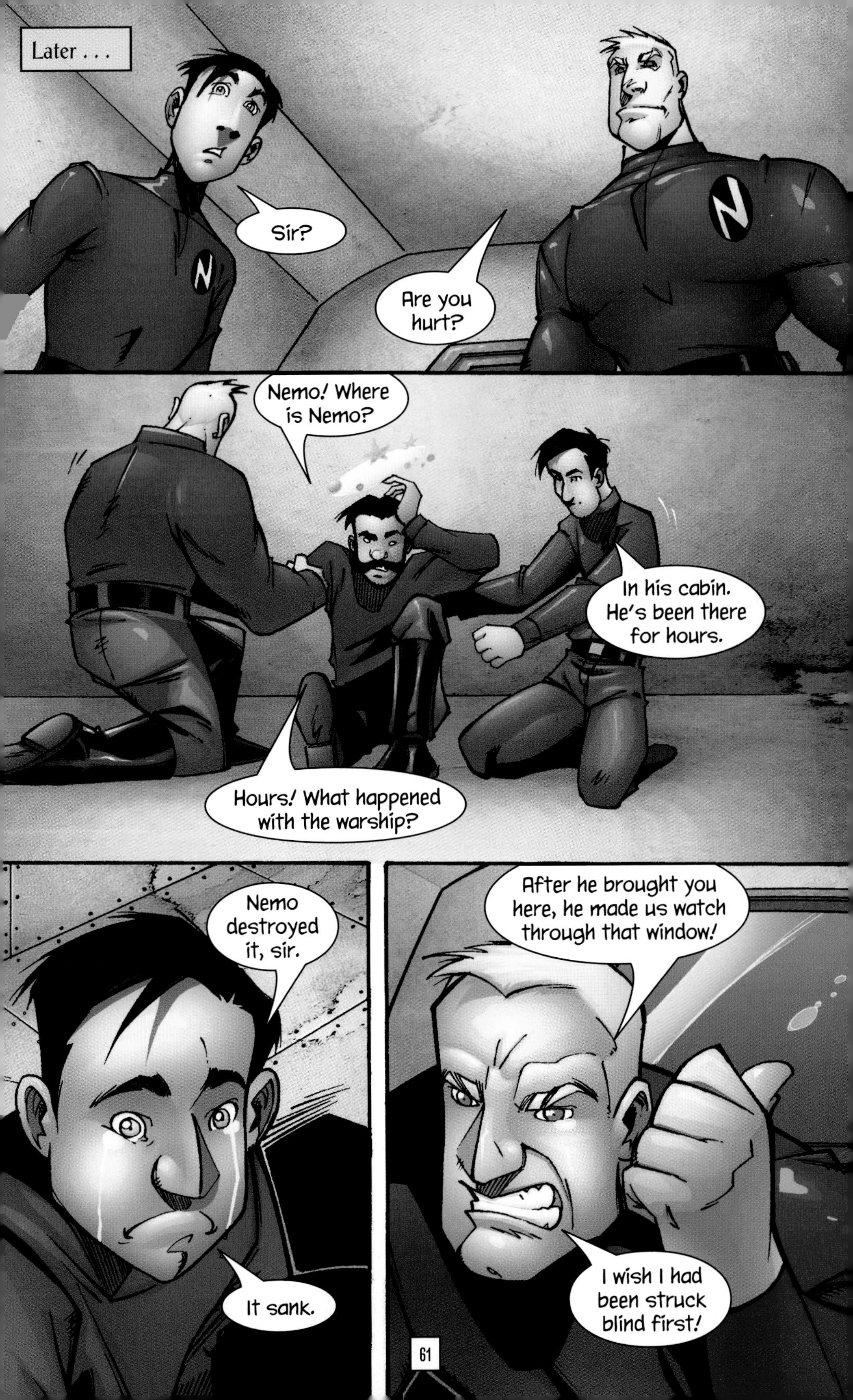
Later . . .
Sir?
Are you hurt?
Nemo! Where is Nemo?
In his cabin. He's been there for hours.
Hours! What happened with the warship?
Nemo destroyed it, sir.
It sank.
After he brought you here, he made us watch through that window!
I wish I had been struck blind first!

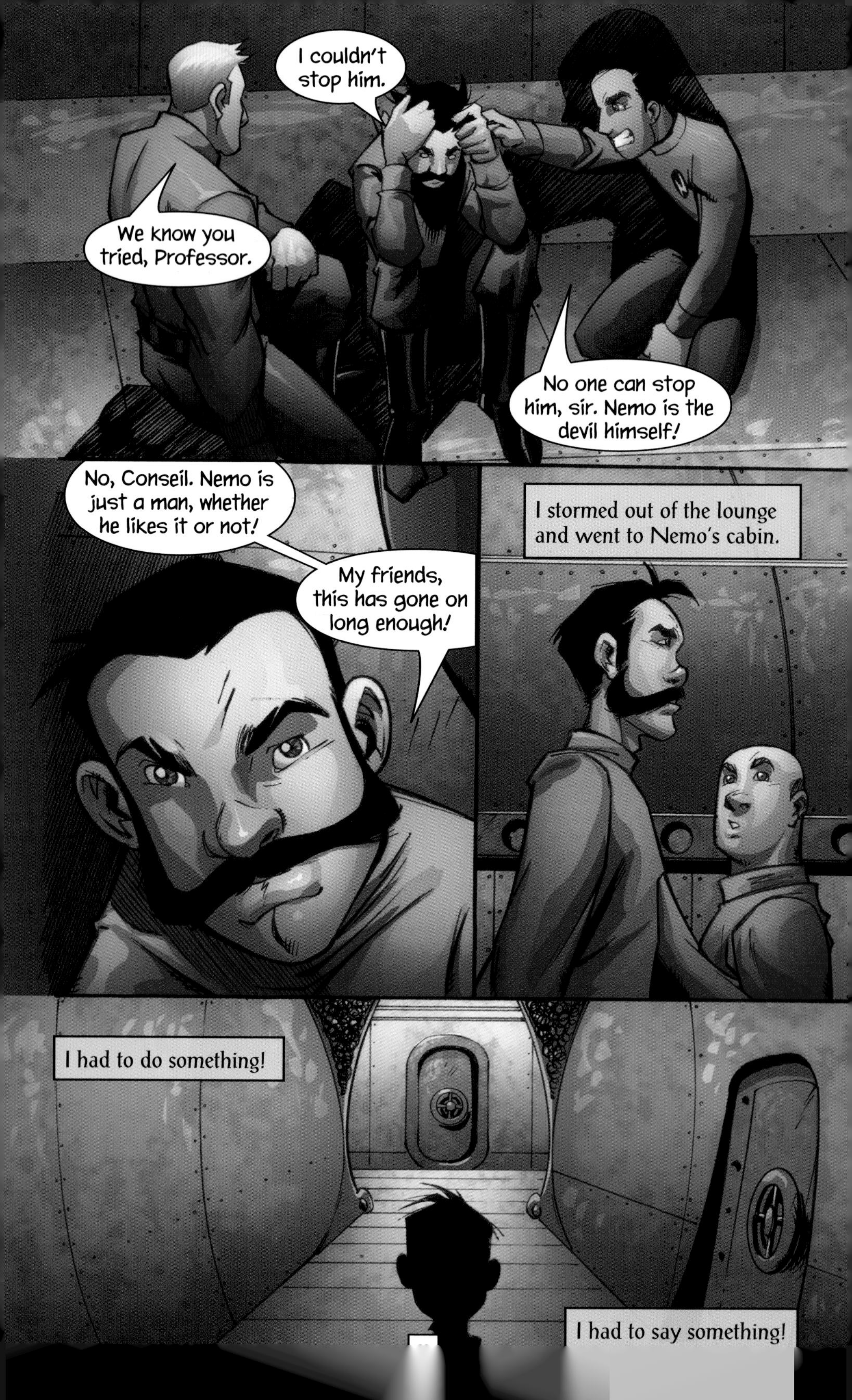
I couldn't stop him.
We know you tried, Professor.
No one can stop him, sir. Nemo is the devil himself!
No, Conseil. Nemo is just a man, whether he likes it or not!
My friends, this has gone on long enough!
I stormed out of the lounge and went to Nemo's cabin.
I had to do something!
I had to say something!

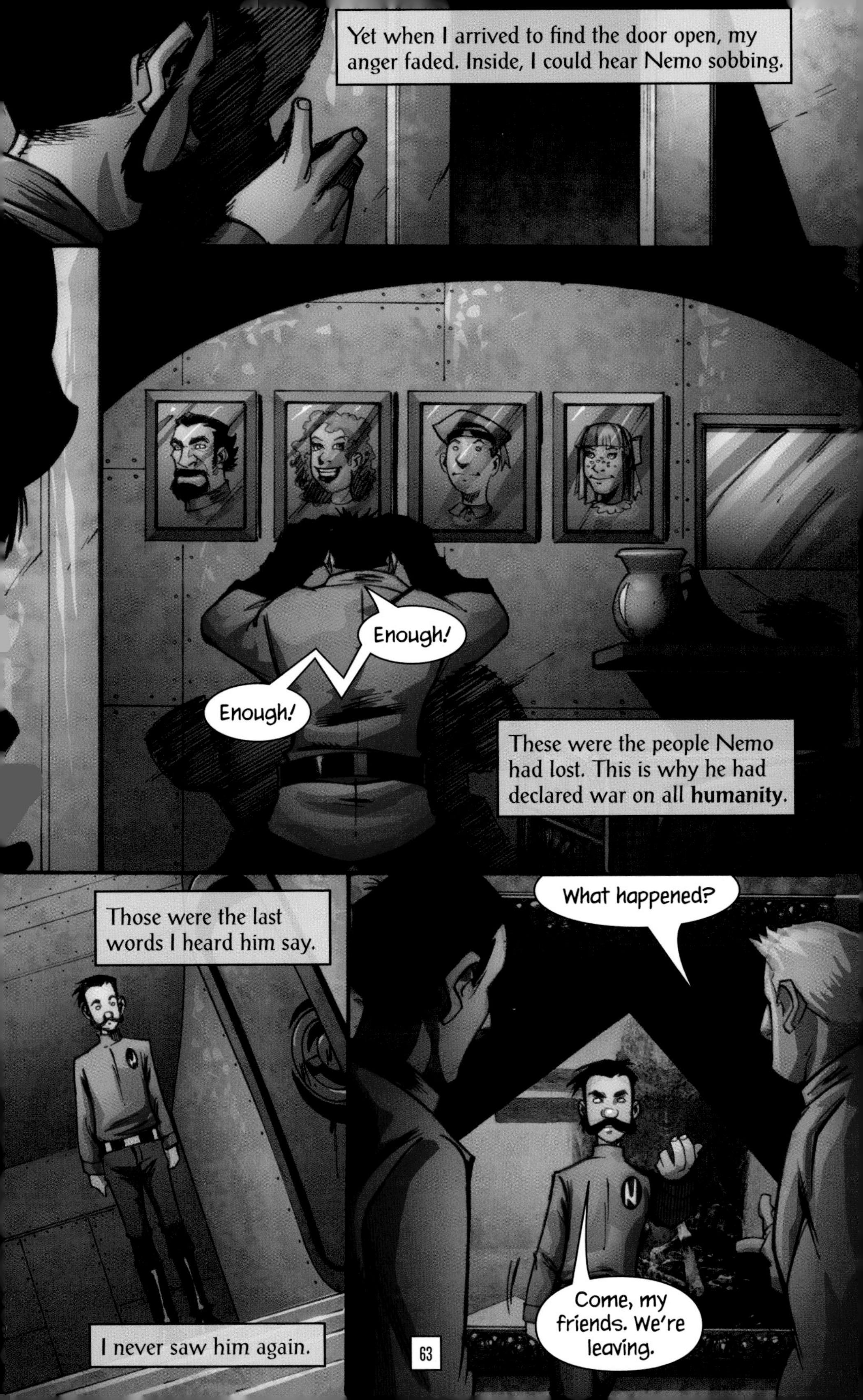
Yet when I arrived to find the door open, my anger faded. Inside, I could hear Nemo sobbing.
Enough!
Enough!
These were the people Nemo had lost. This is why he had declared war on all **humanity**.
Those were the last words I heard him say.
I never saw him again.
What happened?
Come, my friends. We're leaving.

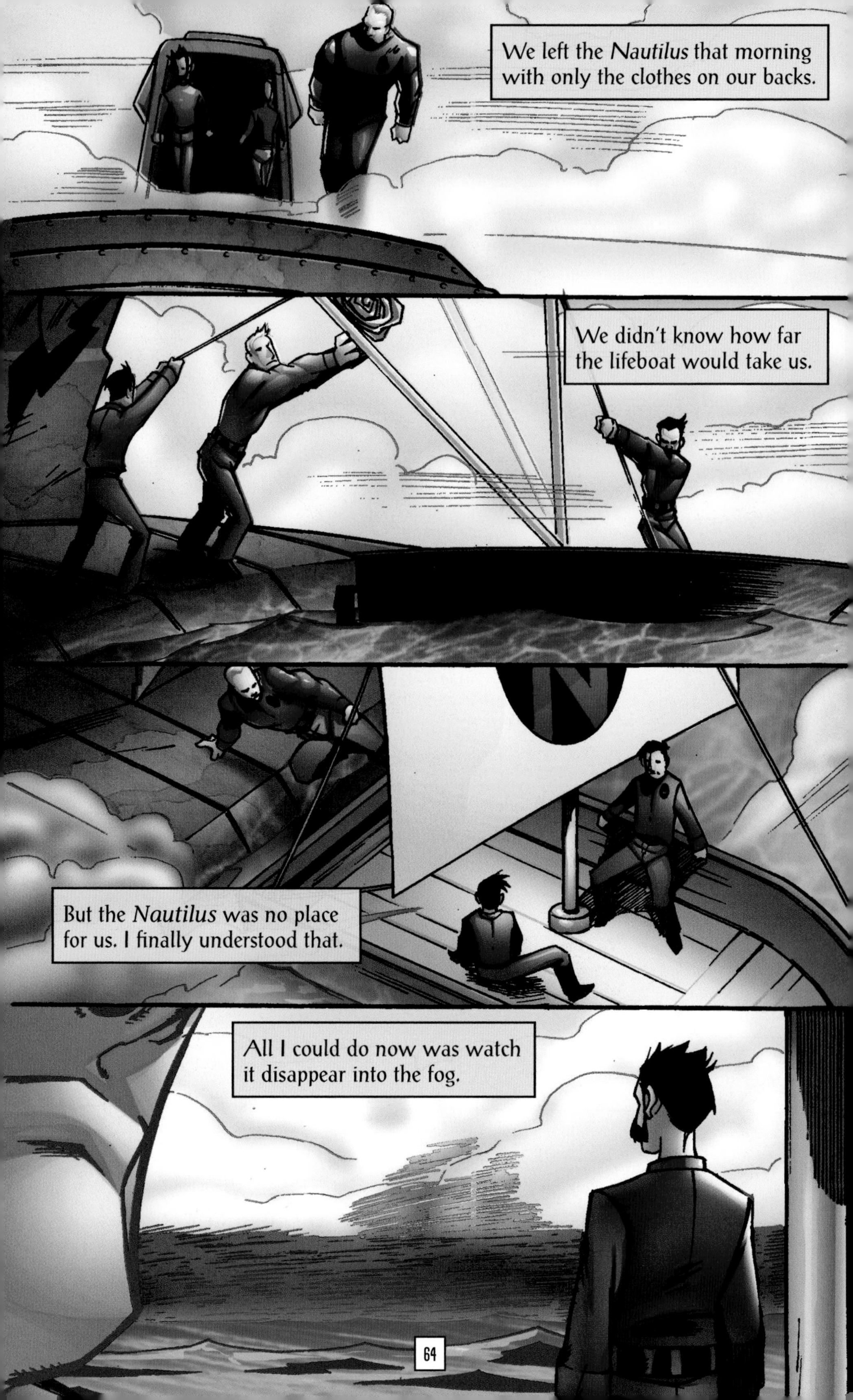
We left the *Nautilus* that morning with only the clothes on our backs.
We didn't know how far the lifeboat would take us.
But the *Nautilus* was no place for us. I finally understood that.
All I could do now was watch it disappear into the fog.

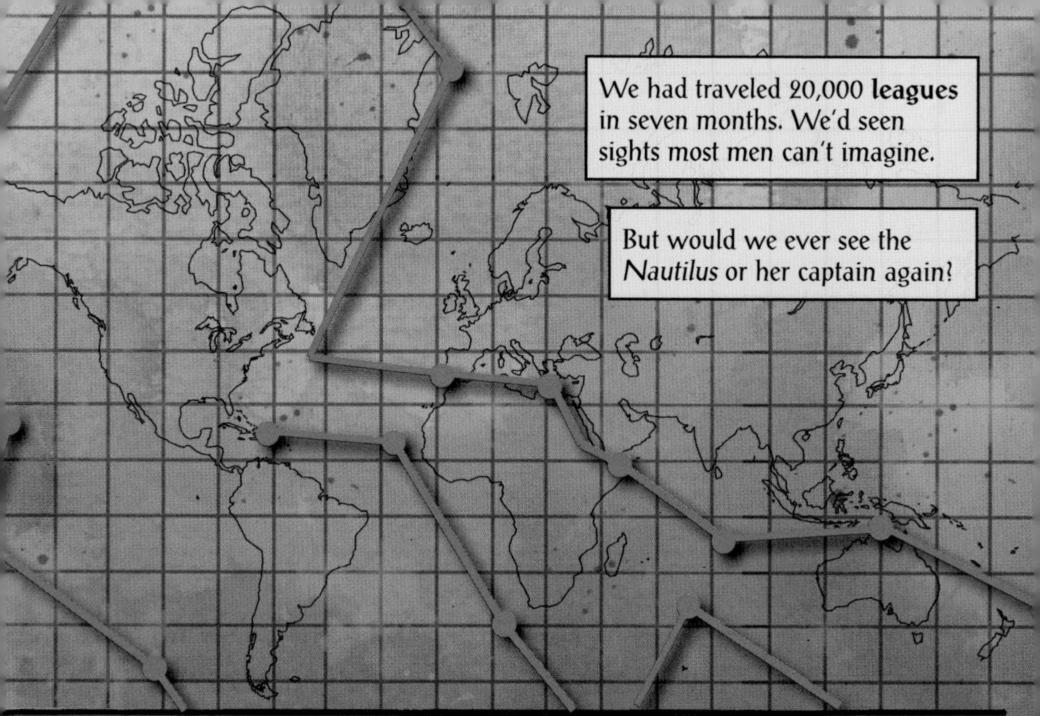
We had traveled 20,000 **leagues** in seven months. We'd seen sights most men can't imagine.
But would we ever see the *Nautilus* or her captain again?

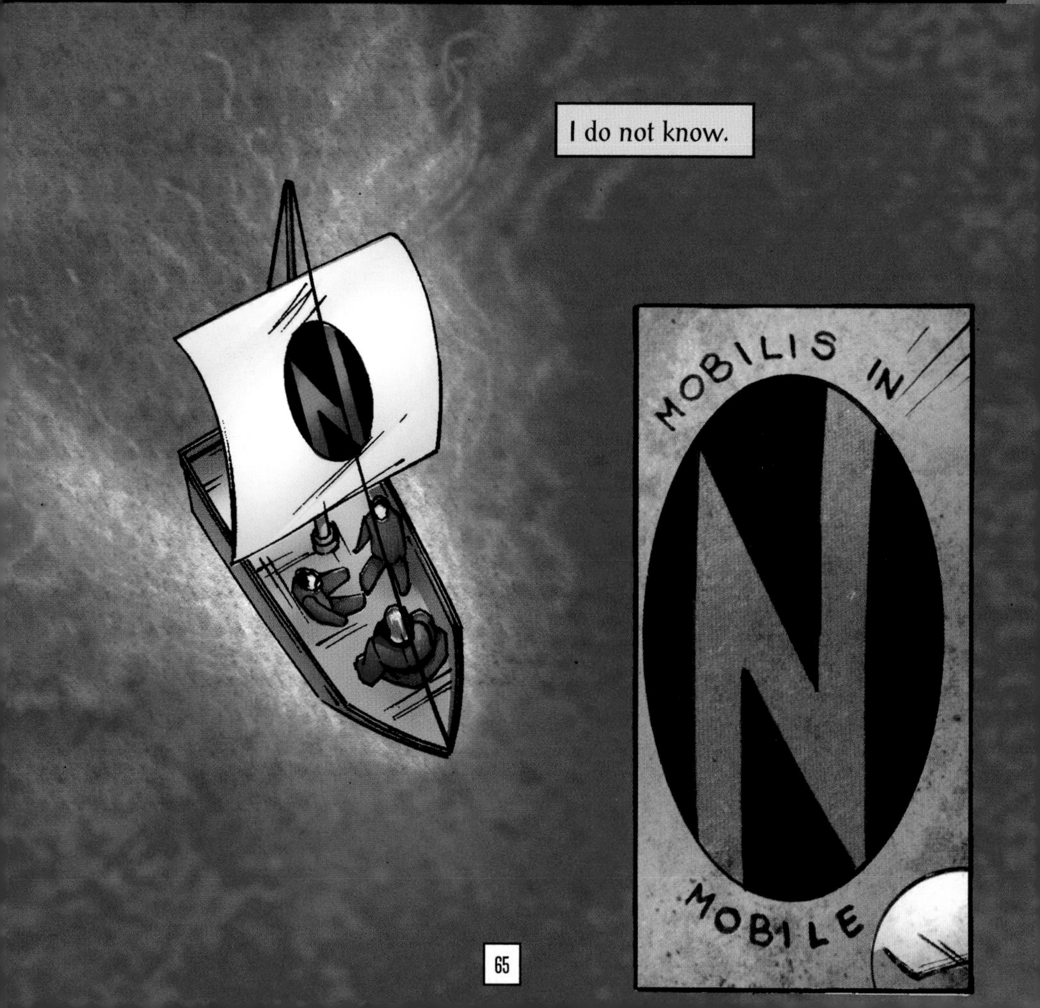
I do not know.
MOBILIS IN MOBILE

ABOUT THE RETELLING AUTHOR AND ILLUSTRATOR

Carl Bowen is a father, husband, and writer living in Lawrenceville, Georgia. He has published a handful of novels, short stories, and comics. For Stone Arch Books and Capstone, Carl has retold *20,000 Leagues Under the Sea* (by Jules Verne), *The Strange Case of Dr. Jekyll and Mr. Hyde* (by Robert Louis Stevenson), *The Jungle Book* (by Rudyard Kipling), "Aladdin and His Wonderful Lamp" (from A Thousand and One Nights), *Julius Caesar* (by William Shakespeare), and *The Murders in the Rue Morgue* (by Edgar Allan Poe). Carl's novel, *Shadow Squadron: Elite Infantry*, earned a starred review from Kirkus Book Reviews.

José Alfonso Ocampo Ruiz was born in 1975 in Macuspana, Tabasco in Mexico, where the temperature is just as hot as the sauce is. He became a comic book illustrator when he was 17 years old, and has worked on many graphic novels since then. Alfonso has illustrated several graphic novels, including retellings of *Dracula* and *Pinocchio*.

GLOSSARY

binoculars (buh-NOK-yuh-lurz)—an instrument people look through to make distant objects appear closer

canal (kuh-NAL)—a passageway that connects two bodies of water

chamber (CHAYM-bur)—a small room or closed-in space

civilized (SIV-i-lized)—having manners and an education

harpoon (har-POON)—a large spear often used to hunt fish or whales

humanity (hyoo-MAN-uh-tee)—all human beings

justice (JUHSS-tiss)—a judge or someone that enforces a set of rules or laws

league (LEEG)—a unit of measurement; one league equals about three miles (five kilometers).

mobilis in mobile (MOH-bee-leess IN MOH-bee-lay)—a Latin phrase meaning "moving through moving waters"

narwhal (NAHR-wol)—a whalelike, ocean animal about 20 feet long with long tusks

theory (THEER-ee)—an idea that explains the reason for something

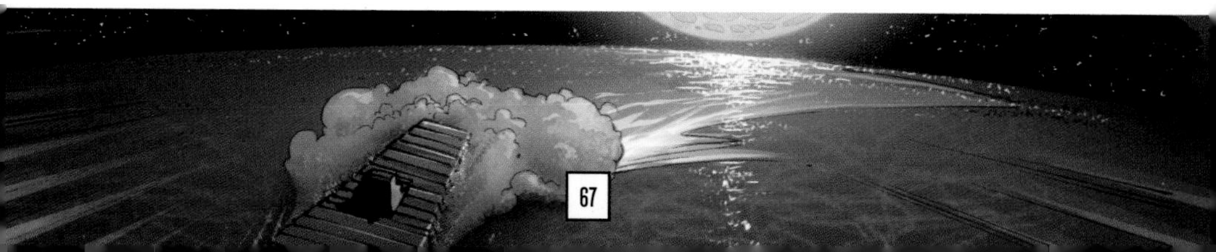

COMMON CORE ALIGNED
READING QUESTIONS

1. **Who is Pierre Arronax? What is his original mission?** *("Refer to details and examples in a text when explaining what the text says.")*

2. **What happens to Pierre Arronax, and how does he end up captured by Captain Nemo?** *("Describe in depth a character, setting, or event in a story.")*

3. **Sanity is a primary theme in this graphic novel. How does the theme of sanity develop in the story? Who in this story is sane, and who is insane? Why?** *("Determine a theme of a story.")*

4. **What is Captain Nemo like? How do you know? Can you find page numbers, pictures, or words to support your explanation?** *("Describe in depth a character . . . drawing on specific details in the text.")*

5. **What does Pierre Aronnax think about Captain Nemo at the beginning of the story? In the middle of the story? And at the end? How does his opinion of Nemo change, and why?** *("Refer to details and examples in a text when explaining what the text says explicitly and when drawing inferences from the text.")*

COMMON CORE ALIGNED
WRITING QUESTIONS

1. **If you were Pierre Aronnax, how would you describe Ned Land?** *("Draw evidence from literary . . . texts to support analysis.")*

2. **Write a letter to your best friend explaining your opinion of the story. Feel free to explore your own thoughts, and cite textual (words or images) examples to support why you feel the way you do. Would you recommend *20,000 Leagues Under the Sea* to a friend?** *("Write opinion pieces on topics or texts, supporting a point of view with reasons and information.")*

3. **Write an informative essay that explains Captain Nemo's development over the course of the story. Does he change? Support your answer using specific examples from the text.** *("Write informative/explanatory texts to examine a topic and convey ideas.")*

4. **If you were a character in the story, who would you be? Why? Be sure to have at least three reasons for your decision.** *("Write narratives to develop real or imagined experiences or events.")*

5. **Describe the *Nautilus*. What does it look like? What can it do? Find images or words to support your description.** *("Draw evidence from literary . . . texts to support analysis.")*

READ THEM ALL!

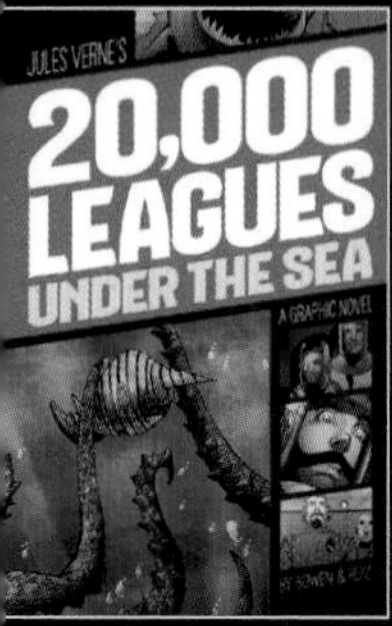
JULES VERNE'S
20,000 LEAGUES UNDER THE SEA
A GRAPHIC NOVEL

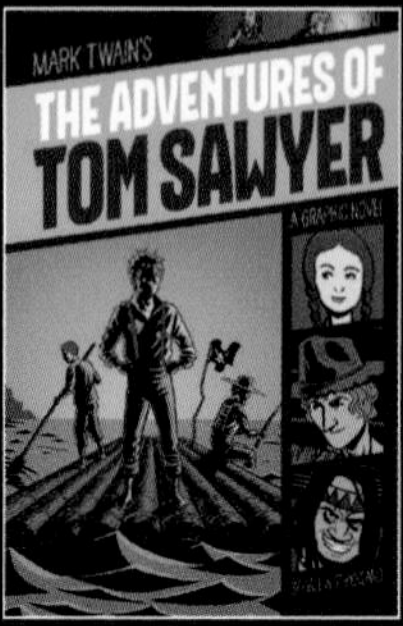
MARK TWAIN'S
THE ADVENTURES OF TOM SAWYER
A GRAPHIC NOVEL

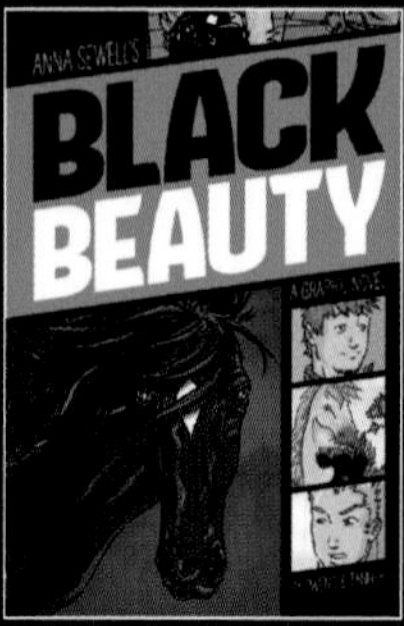
ANNA SEWELL'S
BLACK BEAUTY
A GRAPHIC NOVEL

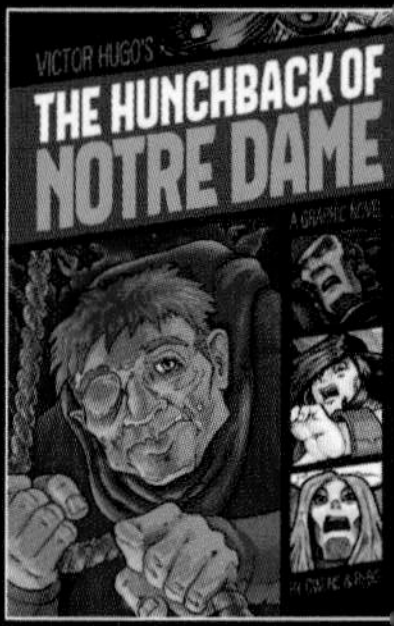
VICTOR HUGO'S
THE HUNCHBACK OF NOTRE DAME
A GRAPHIC NOVEL

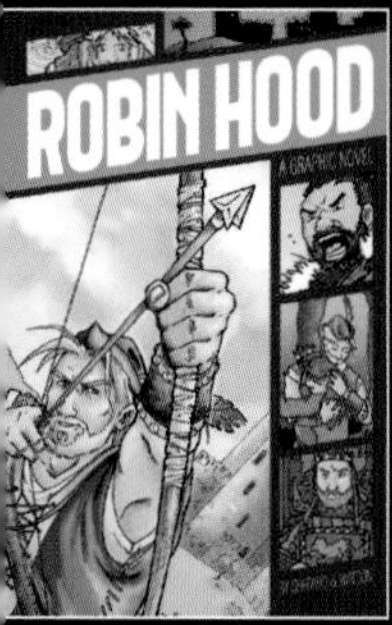
ROBIN HOOD
A GRAPHIC NOVEL

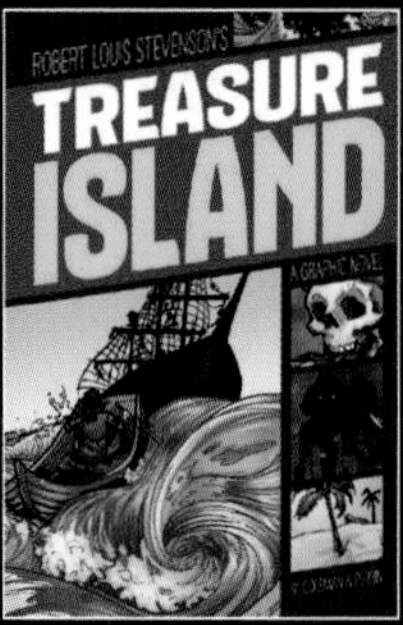
ROBERT LOUIS STEVENSON'S
TREASURE ISLAND
A GRAPHIC NOVEL

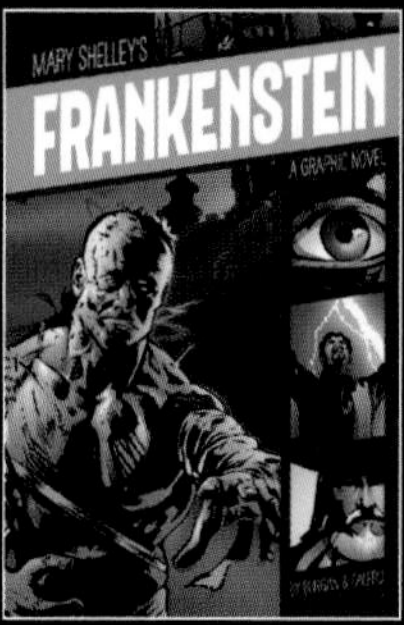
MARY SHELLEY'S
FRANKENSTEIN
A GRAPHIC NOVEL

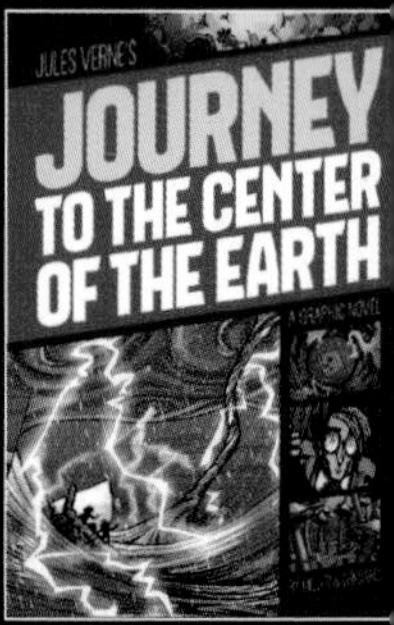
JULES VERNE'S
JOURNEY TO THE CENTER OF THE EARTH
A GRAPHIC NOVEL

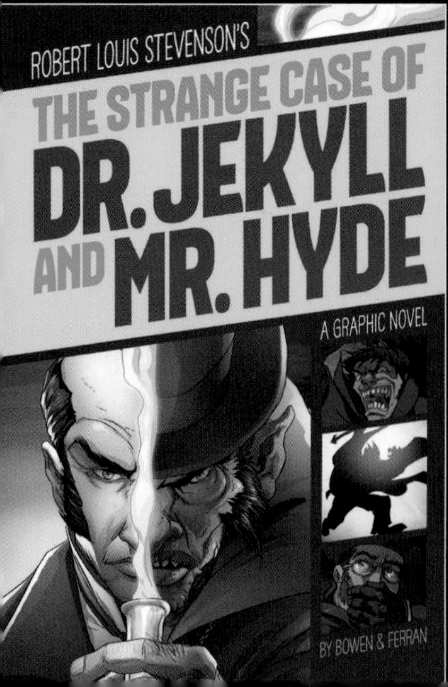
ROBERT LOUIS STEVENSON'S
THE STRANGE CASE OF DR. JEKYLL AND MR. HYDE
A GRAPHIC NOVEL
BY BOWEN & FERRAN

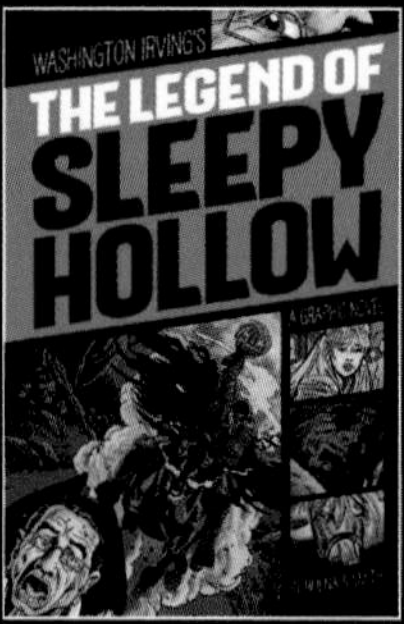
WASHINGTON IRVING'S
THE LEGEND OF SLEEPY HOLLOW
A GRAPHIC NOVEL

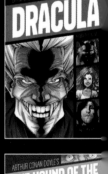

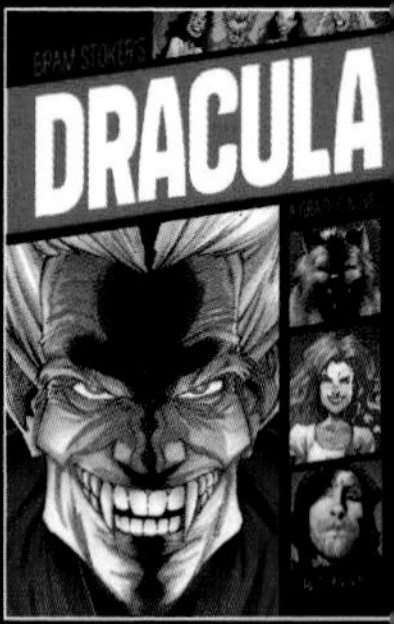
BRAM STOKER'S
DRACULA

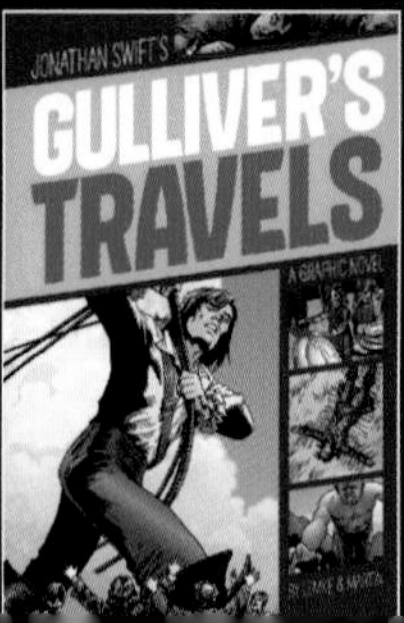
JONATHAN SWIFT'S
GULLIVER'S TRAVELS
A GRAPHIC NOVEL

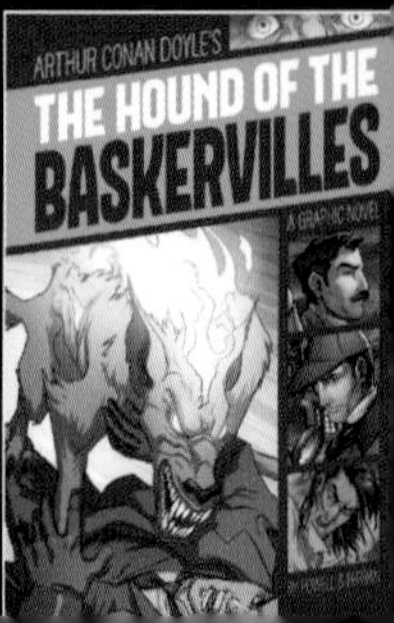
ARTHUR CONAN DOYLE'S
THE HOUND OF THE BASKERVILLES
A GRAPHIC NOVEL

JOHANN DAVID WYSS
THE SWISS FAMILY
ROBINSON
A GRAPHIC NOVEL

**PERSEUS AND
MEDUSA**
A GRAPHIC NOVEL

LEWIS CARROLL'S
**ALICE
IN WONDERLAND**
A GRAPHIC NOVEL

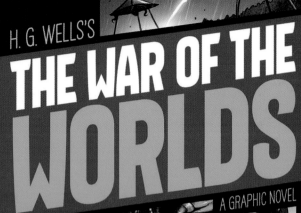

H. G. WELLS'S
THE WAR OF THE
WORLDS

A GRAPHIC NOVEL

BY MILLER & BREVARD

H.G. WELLS'S
THE TIME
MACHINE
A GRAPHIC NOVEL

BY DAVIS & RUIZ

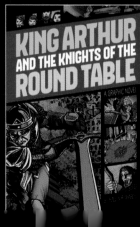

**KING ARTHUR
AND THE KNIGHTS OF THE
ROUND TABLE**
A GRAPHIC NOVEL

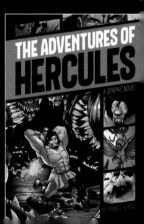

**THE ADVENTURES OF
HERCULES**
A GRAPHIC NOVEL

BY POWELL & RUIZ